Trouble at Mesquite Flats

Soon after his arrival in Mesquite Flats, ex-New York busi-nessman Bodene Rich is committed to Yuma Penitentiary for a vicious assault. Six months later Rich is released, in light of new evidence, and pardoned by Warden Bradley Shaw.

On the day of Rich's release, Shaw hands in his resignation and when he is shot dead on the trail by an unknown gunman, Rich is once again in trouble. Rich finds himself further blighted by circumstance and finds himself working towards a showdown involving a bloody gun battle in open country, where the outcome hangs in the balance until the final shot is fired. . . .

Trouble at Mesquite Flats

Will Keen

A Black Horse Western

ROBERT HALE · LONDON

© Will Keen 2011
First published in Great Britain 2011

ISBN 978-0-7090-9313-8

Robert Hale Limited
Clerkenwell House
Clerkenwell Green
London EC1R 0HT

www.halebooks.com

Typeset by
Derek Doyle & Associates, Shaw Heath
Printed and bound in Great Britain by
CPI Antony Rowe, Chippenham and Eastbourne

PROLOGUE

It was close to three in the afternoon. The sun was a searing disc in skies burned pure white, no longer directly overhead but still hot enough to blister a careless man's exposed skin. Sweat was an irritating snake of moisture crawling down his back beneath the heavy shirt. It trickled from his black, matted hair, trickled into his ears from beneath the damp sweatband of the Stetson he had tipped back to shield his neck, and in the carefully measured intervals when he had tilted his head to drink tepid water from his leather-bound canteen the bitter taste of it was on his lips, its salt sting like liquid fire burning his eyes.

After watching and waiting for six hours that straddled the unbearable heat of high noon, the water he had carefully rationed was now a remembered luxury that caused his dry mouth to cramp painfully, his throat to lock. His own thirst he bore stoically, but several times he had walked the short distance to where his horse was tethered in the relative cool of an overhanging rock outcrop, and allowed it greedily to lap a few ounces of water from his cupped hand. The last time he returned wearily to the rimrock he had drained the canteen as he walked, then angrily cast the empty vessel aside to bounce and clatter down the rocky slope.

To watch without being observed, in a position from which a killing shot could be delivered without conscious effort, he was lying in dust almost too hot to touch, stretched out, belly down. Through the coarse grass sprouting in the gap in the jagged rimrock he looked down from the ridge across a tangled expanse of juniper, prickly pear, rock falls and twisted pine stumps to the road some fifty feet below. The road emerged from between low hills a mile to his right, and traced a sweeping curve below him that saw it swing towards the south into the shimmering heat haze beyond which lay the town of Mesquite Flats.

In the other direction the sluggish ribbon of the Gila River, the town of Yuma and the Arizona State Penitentiary, were hidden by the low hills.

The watcher's pulse quickened unnervingly at the stark mental image of the prison, and the realization of what would certainly befall him if his carefully planned ambush ended in failure brought a lurching sickness to his belly. Suddenly fearful, through slitted eyes he scanned every square inch of terrain in the area where the road emerged from the cleft in the brown, sun-baked hills, looking for movement in the deathly stillness – as he had looked constantly for most of that day.

Still barren emptiness. Still no sign of life.

Without thought, driven by gnawing hatred stoked up by fear of consequences and fury at a man's perceived intrusions into his personal life, his hand moved to the jacket crumpled in the dust at his side. Within its folds, the Winchester rifle lay protected. A necessary precaution. Left out in the stark sunlight for the time he had been lying in ambush, stock and barrel would have become too hot to touch. More importantly, an overheated barrel would have affected the bullet's trajectory, made accurate shooting impossible.

In the encounter that was surely now fast approaching, a weapon in perfect condition was essential even if, since his early youth, a man had been recognized as an expert shot with a rifle.

Savagely, swept by anger, he twisted onto his side and stripped the jacket from the rifle. Then he took the gleaming weapon into his hands and hitched himself well back from the rimrock so that no flash of sunlight on bright metal would reveal his position to the man he was waiting to kill.

He had been meticulous in his planning, and he was meticulous now in the way he checked the rifle. Though covered by the serge cloth, it had been lying in the dust, so he painstakingly checked its oiled working parts for particles of grit that might cause the mechanism to jam. Then he checked that the tubular magazine was full – though he had personally pressed home each shell against the strong spring, and in any case knew deep down that he would need but one shot. Finally, almost lovingly, he worked the lever that inserted a shell into the breech.

The whole procedure took him less than two minutes. That final action, the metallic clack of the shell slamming home, was startlingly loud in the stillness. Yet even as the faint echoes died, deadened by the hot air, several fresh sounds reached him that caused him first to sit bolt upright, then to throw himself flat and wriggle like a snake to his position at the notch in the rimrock.

What he had heard was the distant muffled beating of a horse's hoofs on the dusty road, the musical jingle of harness, the deep tones of a man contentedly singing.

Bradley Shaw, Arizona State Penitentiary's respected warden, was on his way home.

It was Friday. Shaw spent his working week in overall charge of prisoners at the penitentiary, but weekends he worked with his wrangler on his small horse ranch in the Sheep Mountain foothills to the south of Mesquite Flats. The twenty mile trip from the penitentiary to the town and the further five that took him to his ranch were made in a shiny top-buggy pulled by one of his own chestnut mares. It was that top-buggy that was jingling down the slope. Bradley Shaw was making his melodic, oblivious way to a fatal meeting with a .44-.40 bullet.

Coarse grass whispered as the watcher poked the

Winchester's barrel through and tilted it to point down the rugged slope. He wriggled further forward, took several deep breaths; settled. With his left hand he took the weapon's weight; for support he rested the back of his hand lightly on the hot, rough rock. His right hand grasped the pistol grip. His forefinger curled naturally around the trigger. Then, basking in the knowledge that the long hours of waiting were over, he snuggled his cheek against the warm, shiny wood and let his body become still as he peered through the sights.

He had selected his spot carefully. Shaw would pass below him, the top-buggy moving from right to left. Just off the road, several tall green saguaro cactus stood like ancient sentinels in the rough scrub. The watcher had lined the Winchester up on those saguaros, and used them to adjust his sights.

That had been half an hour ago. The top-buggy was now – the watcher lifted his head and squinted up the road, gauging the distance – less than a minute away, no more than fifty yards.

Then, without warning, Shaw's mellow voice broke off as he hauled back on the reins and pulled the top-buggy sideways across the road in a skidding halt. A cloud of choking dust billowed, drifting high in the sunlight. Shaw rose to his feet. Stock still, legs braced and one hand holding the tight leather straps as the top-buggy rocked, his eyes were fixed on the heights.

He's looking straight at me, thought the watcher. He saw a flash of light on the rimrock, is maybe thinking of Apaches but knows damn well it means trouble and is getting ready to flee . . . only he's too damn late.

Bradley Shaw sprang into action. He dropped to a crouch and cracked his whip across the chestnut mare's shoulders. The horse sprang forward. The traces jerked taut, the top buggy lurched into sudden motion, knocking Shaw off balance. Down on one knee, he hung on, his head twisted as he looked fearfully up at the rimrock.

The top-buggy drew level with the saguaros. The watcher squeezed the trigger.

There was a vicious crack as the .44-.40 bullet left the Winchester's muzzle.

On the side of Bradley Shaw's face, a black pockmark appeared. The top-buggy was accelerating rapidly, the frightened mare straining forward with flattened ears and rolling eyes. As if in slow motion, the prison warden fell backwards. Then, as the racing buggy hit a deep rut and bounced onto one wheel, he was thrown sideways out of the flimsy carriage. He landed heavily in the dust, and lay still.

ONE

It was dusk when Bodene Rich rode into Mesquite Flats. He had seen the town's oil lamps winking from afar, seen its buildings sprawling across the desert like flimsy wooden crates spilled chaotically from an overturned wagon. They were painted blood-red by the setting sun, and cast dark shadows that for some reason struck him as sinister.

Maybe, he was to think later, *I should have taken those images as the warning signs they were and given the town a wide berth.*

The main street he rode into was a broad swathe of rutted, hard-packed earth. On either side stood business premises the square false fronts of which bore signs slowly but surely being stripped bare of paint by the hot desert winds. Without being able to see them he knew that on the outskirts of the town there were other streets – First Street, Second Street, and so on – mostly lined on either side by timber homes. Beyond that there were stands of cotton-woods that marked the course of Flats Creek, the

11

river that had made possible the establishment of a town in that desert location. Its source lay somewhere in Sheep Mountain; after a journey of many meandering miles its waters eventually flowed into the much larger Gila River.

Slack in the saddle, enjoying the pleasurable sensation of being astride a horse again, Rich rode with his thoughts firmly fixed on the steak he knew must be sizzling in Millie's café. He was hungry, but his eyes were watchful, and so it was that within thirty seconds all thoughts of his late dinner had been driven clear out of his mind. Instead of anticipating a monster fried meal washed down with black coffee, he was suddenly aware of tension that was like a crackling electric storm hanging over the town. It was an atmosphere with which he was all too familiar. And why shouldn't he be? A prison was fury locked in a cage, the keys held by men with shotguns. For six months he'd lived on his nerves. Tension and fear were emotions he had risen with at dawn each morning and rolled into bed with each night – but here, on a warm evening in Mesquite Flats, those feelings were out of place and unexpected.

The tension seemed to hit him like the prickly heat of an approaching dust storm, washing over him so that his skin tingled as he passed the people, both men and women, who everywhere were standing in small knots.

Watching and waiting, Rich figured, taking careful note of the women's set faces and tight lips, the men's suspicious eyes that followed him as he rode by. Most people would recognize him, Rich knew, but he would not be welcomed. He had ridden into Mesquite Flats as a lean, gun-toting stranger twelve months ago, been escorted out in manacles six months later to begin a five-year sentence in the Arizona State Penitentiary – and now, after just six months, he was back. His sudden reappearance would be a shock that would promote more gossip, lead to more whispering – but it was not why the townsfolk were there. Something else had brought families out onto the warped plank walks, into the shadowed, dusty spaces, had drawn work-weary men to the swing doors of Queenie Hart's Fat Lady saloon with drinks in their hands and menace in their eyes.

This was Arizona, so the plank walks in front of the buildings were mostly shaded by straw or mesquite ramadas. It was under these that the people out on the street had gathered. Conscious of their unremitting scrutiny, Rich rode past Wilson's general merchandise establishment, a grain and feed merchants that bore no name, John Thorpe's bank building with iron bars on its windows and a flimsy door a man could push in with one hand, and the courthouse – this last bringing a thin smile to his lips, for memories of his experiences in that single large room were vivid, and bitter.

He'd been right about the café. Its lighted windows were steamed up, and the haze of blue smoke issuing from the cracks at the top of the door carried with it an enticing aroma of frying food that almost dragged him from the saddle. But for Bodene

Rich, his horse's needs always came first. He steeled himself against the café's raw temptations, rode past the office bearing the name of the lawyer he would forever associate with his own courthouse experiences, then into a wider open space that fronted the livery barn. The earth there was chopped up by horses' hoofs. Rusty horseshoes were scattered around and beneath the old horse trough. A rickety windmill cast a long, ragged shadow.

Something else was there, too, and that something was the centre of attention. It was a top-buggy. Black, well cared for, but now coated with trail dust.

Close to it, men were gathered who were not idly awaiting an event that was yet to happen. It was, Rich suspected, already done and settled in their minds, as inevitable as the next dawn but lacking any of that golden promise. Amongst them he saw the black-suited, bony figure of Ben Laing, the undertaker. His morbid presence added to the cloud of gloom that hung over the gathering. He was standing to one side of the small group, his long face mournful as he talked with obvious gravity to town marshal Dan McReady.

McReady was a grey-haired man in his fifties. He was listening without too much attention to the undertaker, frequently turning his head to stare up the street.

But where, Rich wondered, did the black top-buggy figure in all this?

McReady glared as he recognized the newcomer, then spat into the dust as Rich drew rein and swung down from the saddle.

'What the hell are you doing out of jail?'

'The short answer to that is justice has been done.'

'Justice was done when you were slammed in the calaboose. You attacked Red Booth, a devout Christian, broke both his legs with a mattock hoe. Five years was one tenth of what I would have given, what you deser—'

'I was framed. Everybody knows Booth and his brother homestead on Dieter Bauer's land, close to Flats Creek. Bauer wants them out of there. His foreman drinks hard, fights hard, doesn't waste his breath talking. If you're looking for the truth, then the truth is Bauer sent Al Ferris down to the Booths' place on the creek, knowing damn well how Ferris would handle the encounter.'

'Twelve honest citizens laughed that claim out of the courthouse.'

'They'd spent a whole day listening to a pack of lies.'

'If they were lies, they were backed by facts. You were out of town when Booth was attacked. Liz Carter saw you riding close to his homestead at 'bout the right time. Booth was clubbed to the ground from behind; before he lost consciousness he heard his attacker laughing, mocking him, telling him the fight that started in town ended right there – and a day earlier, you and him got into it outside the Fat Lady.'

'Anyone who saw or heard that argument could have attacked Booth and used it to point the finger at me,' Rich said wearily. 'That was brought out in my defence. The judge admitted it was a possibility.'

'But still you were convicted. You were sentenced to five years, you're out on the street after six months. I could arrest you right now for busting out of the pen,' McReady said tightly. 'I can see you resisting, going for that six-gun, and I'd be praying for that to happen so's I could—'

'He was released early, by order of the warden.'

The slim, dark-suited figure of Spencer Hall had walked up unnoticed. As McReady swung to face him, the lawyer shrugged apologetically. 'Not my doing, Dan. New evidence came to light. Bradley Shaw had no option.'

'How the hell d'you work that out?'

'He called in this morning, decided that as the lawyer who got Rich convicted I should get the news before it became public knowledge.'

'Shaw never did agree with the verdict. If this new evidence backed his opinion he won't have looked at it too closely, so there's still room for doubt.'

'I can't comment on that, but he gave me no details so you'll need to talk to Shaw. But that, and Rich's immediate release, suggests Booth's attacker's got a name now, and that name's not Rich. If that's true, you'll be making an arrest.'

'Trouble is,' Ben Laing said, in his hollow baritone, 'the man carrying that new evidence locked in his head has gone missing.' The undertaker waved a gaunt hand at the top-buggy. 'Shaw's lathered mare brought that through like she had no intention of stopping before Sheep Mountain. George Plant

16

acted real fast. He ran out, grabbed ahold of her and dragged her to a halt.'

Plant, Mesquite Flats' bow-legged hostler, was standing with his backside up against the stone water trough. He said, 'The mare knows me, so it was easy enough to do. Question is, what the hell set her running?'

'She was spooked,' McReady said flatly. 'I'll lay odds it was the sound of gunfire.'

The lawyer was keenly watching McReady. 'You think Shaw's dead?'

'Yes I do, and I think he was shot by Bodene Rich. Look at the timing. Shaw's buggy rolls into town, empty, and within the hour this fellow shows up bold as brass.'

'Prisoners due for release are out of there early in the morning. Shaw always stays until business is finished for the day.'

'So Rich left before him, picked his spot high up on some ridge and settled down for a long wait. Hell, he didn't even need to keep watch, he'd have heard Shaw's goddamn warbling a mile off—'

'Wagon coming.'

Vern Brown, a deputy who'd been posted across the street, was walking over. As he did so, Rich heard the murmur of voices. People away to the left were surging out from the shelter of the ramadas. He listened to unseen wheels rumbling over the street's hard ridges, the musical jingle of harness and, moments later, a buckboard hove into view with two men up front. One wore a badge. It gleamed in the

17

fading light.

'Body in the back under that canvas,' Ben Laing said in a voice laden with doom.

The buckboard veered away as it came level with the men gathered by the water trough, heading for the marshal's office and jail fifty yards away on the other side of the street. But McReady called out and waved. The deputy at the reins applied the brake, then swung team and buckboard towards the livery barn in a drifting cloud of dust.

'Damn near threw Bradley into the street,' George Plant marvelled.

'If it's him,' Hall said.

'Who the hell else could it be?' McReady growled, and the lawyer glanced quickly at Bodene Rich as if for enlightenment.

Feeling strangely detached, Rich watched McReady walk to the the rear of the buckboard, lean over and lift the edge of the canvas. The marshal nodded, to nobody in particular, then let the canvas fall and returned to the group. He walked right up to Rich and stood with his big fists planted on his hips. His chin was thrust forward belligerently, and there was fury in his blue eyes.

'I can't arrest you for breaking jail, but give me one good reason why I shouldn't arrest you for the cold-blooded murder of Bradley Shaw.'

'Because I didn't do it.'

'You're carrying a rifle.' McReady jerked his head towards Rich's horse. 'If I look at it and it's been fired—'

'It has. I'd been in jail six months. The feel of a horse beneath me was pleasurable. I wanted to experience the hard kick of a rifle against my shoulder, and there was a convenient rattler, basking in the sun.'

'At any other time that'd be a good story. But this is not any other time, this is now, and a good man's lying dead in that wagon. Bodene Rich—'

'Wait.'

Hall, the lawyer, had moved forward. He couldn't get between the two men, but his sharp command forced McReady back a pace.

'Think before you act, Dan,' the lawyer said. 'If Shaw had evidence that set Rich free, why would he kill the man?'

'Right now I'm not looking for reasons, I'm looking for a cowardly bushwhacker.'

'Yeah, but Rich has rode into town, Pa.' The deputy at the reins was leaning forward with his elbows on his knees as he listened. 'Would he be likely to do that if he'd gunned down Shaw?'

'I repeat my advice,' Hall said, glancing gratefully across at his son. 'Wait, Dan. If Shaw released Bodene Rich, it's likely that he told somebody under him why he was doing it. You can find that out by riding to Yuma tomorrow. Or, if you're too busy, send Pete.'

'What about him?' McReady's jaw muscles were bunched as he gestured at Rich. 'Far as I'm concerned, he's guilty of the attack on Booth and Shaw's murder until something tells me different – but by the time Pete gets back from Yuma he could be cross-

19

ing the border into Mexico.'

'I'm going nowhere,' Rich said.

'Damn right, you're not,' McReady said, and as he reached a decision his grin was savage. 'I'm holding you on suspicion, Rich. You can cool your heels in one of my cells until this mess is cleared up.'

TWO

Dieter Bauer was at the table finishing a meal of cold beef and potatoes washed down with black coffee that twisted his face into an ugly grimace of distaste when Kris banged open the door and stamped in out of the rain. He watched his son slap his Stetson against his thigh, then sling it blindly onto one of the worn easy chairs, and for some reason the look in his son's eyes gave him immediate cause for concern.

Something, Dieter, figured, had gone badly wrong, and he had enough on his mind without Kris adding to his troubles.

'Bradley Shaw's dead.'

'Well, hallelujah to that,' Dieter said. 'About time somebody up and plugged the philandering old bastard.' He widened his eyes, fork poised over his plate. 'I take it that is what happened? His heart didn't give out when he was in the hotel entwined with one of his buxom lady friends?'

'You mean Ma?'

'Your ma ain't buxom, and you can take it any

21

damn way you like,' Dieter said, and the fork clattered onto his plate as he pushed it away. 'So tell me, what did happen?'

'He was ambushed, 'bout four miles out of town. McReady sent his son out lookin' when Shaw's mare clattered in pulling the empty top-buggy.'

Dieter was at the stone fireplace, packing his pipe with rough black tobacco. 'A former con's paid him back for his tender ministrations in the sweltering confinement of the Yuma Pen,' he said, and cocked an eye at his son. 'Nothing wrong with that, done us all a favour – so why the concern?'

'Bodene Rich is back in town.'

'Rich?' Dieter's mouth dropped open. He closed it, dragged his hand across his face, then frowned and shook his head. 'Rich is doing five years for turning Red Booth into a cripple. What the hell are you talking about?'

'I was drinking in Queenie Hart's when Shaw's buggy bounced in. I wandered over to the livery. McReady was there, a few others. They were talking when Rich came riding down the street.'

There was a wooden stool by the fireplace. Dieter sank down onto it, leaned back against the stone. He applied a match to his pipe, squinted through the smoke at Kris.

'Talking about what?'

'Before Rich arrived, I don't know. After, McReady wanted to arrest Rich for breaking out of the pen. That Fancy Dan lawyer told him to hold his horses, something about the warden having new evidence that said Rich didn't touch Red Booth.'

'Now I wonder where Shaw got ahold of that?' Dieter said softly. He sucked pensively on his pipe, his eyes distant, then fixed his son with a searching gaze. 'And why it's got you all hot and bothered?'

For a moment Kris didn't answer. He shucked his jacket and sent it towards the chair to fall soggily on his wet hat, dragged his fingers through his long dark hair. There was a bottle of whiskey on the dresser. He poured himself a drink, raised the glass questioningly to his father, received a negative shake of the head.

Kris leaned back against the dark oak, drank, pursed his lips.

'If Rich didn't break Red's legs,' he said, 'somebody else did.'

'So? If it wasn't you, why get in a lather?'

'It wasn't me.'

'I know that. But you're acting mighty strange.'

'If he got it wrong the first time—'

'Who?'

'McReady. Or Hall, the lawyer. I don't know.' Kris shrugged. 'But whoever it was, they can make the same mistake again. That means every man who can't account for his whereabouts on that day and at that time is going to be shaking in his boots.'

'I wouldn't put it that strong,' Dieter said.

'That's because everybody knows you were laid up with a busted arm. You're clear. Me, hell, I don't know where I was—'

He broke off as the door banged open and a big

23

man in a slicker came in out of the rain. He stopped there, dripping; held the door part closed behind him, looked around the room and then directly at Dieter.

'Mrs Bauer not here?'

'I don't know where my wife is, Al. Why?'

'This month's a week old, and the boys are still waiting for last month's pay. They're worried. I know your wife handles the accounts, so. . . .'

'She's picking up the cash from the bank tomorrow. When she gets back I'll come over to the bunkhouse and pay them personally.' He stabbed his pipe at his son. 'Kris tells me Bodene Rich is out of jail. You heard anything?'

Al Ferris had the broken nose and scarred eyebrows of a bar-room brawler. There was nothing behind his cold grey eyes when, after a fleeting moment's cogitation, he shook his head.

'Just letting you know so's you can dig back through six months of memories to find your original statement.' Dieter nodded slowly, watching for a reaction from his big foreman. 'As I recall, Al, you were the number one suspect for the attack on Red before McReady got fixated on Bodene Rich.'

'Bradley Shaw is dead,' Dieter Bauer said.

Still sitting on the stool with his drink, he was watching his wife, Ellie, as she stood before the mirror and used her slender fingers to tease her long dark hair into shape. She was ten years younger than his fifty-four years, a slim and shapely woman who

24

was physically strong enough to hold Dieter off when he attacked her with his fists, mentally strong enough to have endured twenty years of a flawed marriage and remain unscathed in mind and body.

Dieter saw her pause. Her damp hair was twisted about her fingers. In the mirror, he could see her face. Her dark-brown eyes had widened, and were watching him. There was a stillness in the room. She had caught her bottom lip between her teeth – but she often did that, and it could mean anything, or nothing. Then she took a breath, gave her hair a final fluff and turned to face him.

'That's not where I've been.'

'I didn't say it was.'

'Liz Carter's pregnant. She wanted some advice.'

'Which you are qualified to give. Having borne a child yourself, what, nineteen years ago?'

'Or perhaps I just went there to get away from you,' Ellie Bauer said.

'No.' Dieter shook his head. 'I didn't put it into words, but we both know where you went. You've been sniffing around Bradley Shaw's place over there in the foothills. He didn't come home. You hung around in the rain, gave up when you figured he'd stopped off in the Flats and got tied up with something younger, more tasty.'

'Think what you like.'

'I always do. Right most of the time, too.' He flicked a finger against his empty glass, listened to the sharp ting. 'Don't you want to know the rest? Hear the bit that spooked your son?'

'Where is he?'

'In bed.'

'The best place. Anything coming out of your mouth is either lies, or garbage, and Kris's a fool to listen.'

'This came from Kris. He was in town.'

'Be more specific. He was holding up the bar in the Fat Lady saloon. Have you noticed how he's been spending more and more time in there over the past months?' She looked at him speculatively. 'If you're right most of the time, let me hear your thoughts on that. Why has your son turned to drink, Dieter? What's eating away at that young man's insides?'

'He was down at the livery barn, Ellie, watching and listening while Marshal Dan McReady did his best to deal with a situation that rocked him back on his heels.'

'Take a lot to do that to that cocksure gentleman.' She smiled crookedly. 'I suppose you'd better tell me what's going on.'

He shook his head. 'Got a better idea. I'll let you stew. You'll find out tomorrow when you collect the cash from the bank.'

'Ah.' She nodded. 'Al's been in, complaining.'

'Justifiably. Maybe now Shaw's out of the picture you'll have more time for ranch affairs.' His voice had tightened. The big fists she knew so well were clenched. 'In the meantime, you'd better think about what you've been telling him, and hope those lies have gone with him to the grave.'

'However much you might deny it, Dieter, what-

26

ever has died with him was the truth. Sit there and contemplate on that while you drink the night away. I'm going to bed.'

THREE

McReady let Bodene Rich out of jail at dawn the next day. Sent him out into a street veiled by the hanging mist that presaged the usual Arizona day of dry, energy-sapping heat.

He set him free, but sent him out unarmed.

'I reckon I'll hang on to six-gun and rifle,' the marshal said. 'Time spent in the pen can turn a good man bad, make an already wicked man pure poison. Spencer Hall put you inside. I'd hate him to end up with two broken legs.'

'If that was my intention,' Rich said, 'holding on to my guns won't stop me. You should be thinking about the men out there who believe I did that to Red Booth. He's got a brother. You were in that courtroom, you heard his threats.'

'You should have thought of that,' McReady said, 'before you rode back into Mesquite Flats.'

He was standing in the doorway, thumbs hooked in his belt. Rich was on the plank walk, shaded by the ramada but feeling the early morning sun breaking through the mist to warm his back. As he took critical note of the look in McReady's eyes, he was gripped by tension. Sending him out as good as naked was linked to the early release, and he knew damn well he didn't have to remind the marshal of the men out there who hated his guts.

Whatever was going to happen he realized, with a sick foreboding, had its beginnings when Dan McReady took him off the street and locked him in a cell.

Rich shook his head, turned away and stepped down off the plank walk. It was a longish stroll across the street to Plant's livery barn. The mist was lifting, which gave him some relief: he would see trouble coming. But because at that time of day few people were about, if trouble did come he would get no help.

Probably wouldn't get help, he thought ruefully, even if the street was crowded.

He was halfway across the dusty expanse when he heard a scrape, and a metallic clatter. Rich shot a glance to his right. John Thorpe, white-haired, was unlocking his bank's flimsy door. Further up the street, Queenie Hart was standing in the doorway of the Fat Lady. The red dress hanging loose over her ample figure was a flash of colour. She lifted a hand. Rich thought it was in greeting. Then he realized she was pointing.

But where?

He had almost reached the horse trough when the three men made their move. Two emerged from the livery barn, walking out from the shadows beyond the open double doors into the brightening sunlight. Rich didn't know them. He guessed they were drifters, or men from the bigger town of Yuma. The taller of the two was looking at him and grinning. The other was looking across the street.

When Rich flashed a glance behind him, he saw Frank Booth stepping down from the plank walk fronting the jail.

Damn fellow was hiding in a nearby doorway, waiting for me to come out, he thought. McReady knew it, had a hand in it, and was laughing at me.

He turned to face the frontal threat. Both men were advancing in a leisurely manner. Bodene Rich was going nowhere. No help was at hand. They had no need to hurry.

Rich lifted his hands.

'I'm unarmed, outnumbered three to one. I'd have more respect for you if you threw away your six-guns.'

'The respect of a convicted criminal is not something to improve my day,' Frank Booth said.

Rich didn't turn. The homesteader's voice was closer, but there was unexplained breathlessness in it. He's tense, Rich thought, wound up as tight as a drum. What he's doing is out of character. He figures making me pay for crippling his brother is what's expected of him, but it goes against his nature. Defending himself would justify violence, but attacking an unarmed man would go against his Christian beliefs and seriously damage his self respect. So, remember the man's behind you, and dangerous, but worry about the others.

They'd split up and were coming at him around the ends of the horse trough. The tall man was still grinning as he punched one gloved fist into the palm of the other hand. The shorter, stockier man bent as he came between horse trough and windmill. He scooped up a hefty baulk of wood, held it in both hands like a baseball bat.

There go my legs, Rich thought.

The tall man was almost on him. Booth's footsteps could be heard scuffing the street's packed earth; he was hanging back. The man with the timber was closing on Rich, but watching his colleague.

That lean fellow's the leader, Rich thought. If I give him the chance, he'll make the first move. Then the others will be on me.

In one swift movement he picked up a heavy horseshoe, stepped forward and smashed it edge-on across the tall man's unshaven face. The rusty metal ripped a jagged gash across his forehead. He staggered backwards, clapped his hands to his face. A red tide of blood flowed between his fingers.

The stocky man braced himself. Knuckles white, he swung the heavy timber at Rich's head. Rich ducked under it. The wild swing threw the man off balance. Rich stepped close, drove his knee hard into the man's groin. He gasped doubled up. Rich ripped the timber from his grasp and kneed him in the face. He heard the crunch of a broken nose, stepped away and kicked him in the ribs as he went down.

31

But now Booth had his justification. Rich heard the rapid drumming of his boots. He dropped the timber, spun, slammed his left fist backhand into the advancing homesteader's face. Booth's eyes rolled. His legs buckled. Rich grabbed him as he went down. One hand clamped on the man's heavy leather belt, the other on his collar. Rich picked him up, swung him around and dumped him face down in the horse trough.

Booth went under with a splash. Filthy water surged, washed over the edges of the trough. The dazed man lying among the rusty horseshoes gasped, spluttered. Out of the corner of his eye Rich saw the tall man with the bloody face coming back at him. He released Booth's belt, shifted that hand to a point between the man's shoulder blades, and pushed down hard.

'Back off,' he said, 'or this man drowns.'

'Before he drowns,' the tall man snarled, 'you die,' and his bloody, gloved right hand swept his six-gun out of its holster.

'Hold it right there,' a level voice said, and there was the unmistakable sound of a shotgun being cocked. George Plant, the hostler, was standing in the doorway of his livery barn. The shotgun held steady on the tall man.

Bodene Rich took a deep breath. He lifted Frank Booth out of the trough, stood him upright, then stepped away. The homesteader slumped soggily to the ground, breath bubbling. Rich turned and looked back across the street.

32

In the doorway of the jail, Dan McReady was casually smoking a cigarette.

'My advice,' McReady said, 'would be to leave Mesquite Flats in a hurry.'

Rich buckled on his gunbelt, let the Winchester that had been returned to him with his six-gun rest muzzle-down in the crook of his arm.

'Perhaps I'll do that,' Rich said. 'After all, most people do, from time to time. They come and go. The town's a convenience.'

'For you, it's an inconvenience. You've just looked into your future.'

'No. If you'd been watching, you'd have seen three hard men staring death in the face as their lives flashed before their eyes. But as we're talking about convenience, I'd say you were conveniently looking the other way. I wonder why? Whose thumb are you under, McReady? Who's slipping you greenbacks on the quiet?'

A couple of badged deputies were walking up the plank walk on their way to work. One was McReady's boy, the man who'd brought in Warden Bradley's Shaw's body. They caught what Rich was saying, and stared hard at him before turning into the jail.

'Pete's riding to Yuma Pen to find out if the warden shared this new evidence he'd got hold of,' McReady said, ignoring the insult. 'It got you out of jail, but it's possible Shaw died before doin' any talking. Either way, I don't care. You're trouble, and I want you out of my town.'

'So now it's your town?'

'My town, as in I'm responsible for law and order.' McReady shook his head as if baffled, flicked the stub of his cigarette into the street. 'Where do you hail from, Rich? Who are you? What the hell are you doing in Mesquite Flats?'

'You know where I'm from, you know my name. If you'd asked me what I'm doing here before I walked into Shaw's office in the Yuma Pen this time yesterday morning, I'd have struggled to answer. Ten minutes later, when I walked out of there a free man, the answer was in my pocket.'

McReady stared, now clearly puzzled. 'Release papers? Signed by the warden? You don't get a copy – and they'd tell me how you got out of Yuma, not what you're doing here in Mesquite Flats.'

But before he'd got halfway through explaining his confusion, he was talking to Rich's back.

As he'd glanced away, tired of talk that was going nowhere, Rich had seen Spencer Hall unlocking the door to his office. Now he stepped down off the plank walk and headed diagonally across the street.

'You open for business, Hall?' he called.

Hall glanced across at McReady who was still outside the jail, then back at Rich.

'I saw what happened. The end of it. Are you pressing charges for assault against Booth and his companions? Or lodging a complaint against the town marshal?'

'Neither of those,' Rich said. 'Step inside and tend to the coffee pot. I'll be with you before you've got

34

two cups poured.'

He changed direction, and went into the cool, shaded interior of the livery barn. The night before, he had paid George Plant to look after his horse for as long as he was in jail, and hung his rig on a rail with the other saddles. Now he leaned the Winchester against the rail, unbuckled a saddle-bag and took out a flat brown envelope. With that in his hand he went out into the dazzling sunlight that was already sucking moisture out of the air and turning the dust hot underfoot, and made his way to the lawyer's office.

In an atmosphere thick with the scent of polished wood and the smoke from expensive cigars, Hall was standing behind his desk shuffling papers. Bodene Rich looked around, sniffed, then grinned. No steaming cups. No smell of hot coffee. The lawyer didn't consider him that important. Well, he was in for a shock.

'So what do you want?' Hall said. He sat down, smiled patronizingly. 'If it's not legal action against your attackers, or McReady, then I suppose you're seeking compensation for wrongful imprisonment—'

'I've got a letter from Bradley Shaw. Addressed to you. Concerning me.'

Hall stared. 'Shaw's dead.'

'Yeah. He wrote this before he died.'

'Very funny. What I meant was that I thought, in the circumstances, I'd received my last communication from the warden.'

'You were wrong.'

Rich dropped into the chair reserved for clients and placed the envelope on the desk. Spencer Hall picked it up, looked at his name written on the front in a bold hand, and carefully slit it open with a horn-handled paper knife. He slipped out folded paper that to Rich looked like expensive cream vellum, and began to read. As he did so, his face lost all expression. The letter was quite short, but Hall read through it twice. When he'd finished he carefully folded the paper. Still holding it, he leaned back in his chair, frowning.

'If he hadn't been murdered,' he said slowly, 'Shaw was resigning his job and heading back East, accompanied by someone for whom he has great affection. Do you know anything of that?'

'No,' Rich lied. 'But what you've just told me gives a reason for the bit that comes next.'

'He wants me to expedite the sale of his Sheep Mountain property, and all that goes with it.' Hall paused, pursed his lips, tapped them thoughtfully with the folded paper. 'He names you as the purchaser,' he said softly.

Rich nodded. 'Yes, he does.'

'That can't be right. He also names a price a man like you cannot possibly afford.'

'You get started sorting out the legal papers needed to complete the deal, you'll have the money on your desk before the ink's dry.'

'I don't believe it. How can you possibly—'

'That, and much more, arrived in John Thorpe's bank by wire transfer on the same day I rode into

Mesquite Flats twelve months ago.'

Hall had begun to sweat, and Rich could under-stand why. The man sitting in his client's chair was the same man he had sent to Yuma Penitentiary for a vicious assault. Suddenly that man's status was about to change, and that change would create confusion: the convict scratching around for nickels and dimes to buy his next drink would become a wealthy landowner, but he was still Bodene Rich. If the reason for his early release from Yuma had died with Bradley Shaw, he would be walking under a cloud of suspicion. As it was, the people of Mesquite Flats were still convinced he had attacked Red Booth, and reviled him for it; and Marshal Dan McReady would be happy to convict him of the murder from ambush of the prison warden.

Flustered, Hall said, 'This sale is not as simple as you make out.'

'I don't make anything out. Shaw's dead, he's named me as buyer.'

'If there is no will, property goes to next of kin.'

'You're his lawyer. The words you've just used tell me you know there is no will, and Shaw himself told me he was alone in the world.'

'The unusual circumstances—'

'Doc Flint issued a death certificate late last night. Circumstances don't change facts. How he died cannot affect this sale.'

'Shaw was shot down from ambush. If you were the man who. . . .'

Hall's voice trailed off. He'd seen the look on

37

Rich's face; he seemed to shrink back in his chair.

'In that cabinet over there, Mr Hall, you will have ready-printed legal papers,' Rich said softly. 'My name goes on the top of one of those relating to property sales, Shaw's authorized you to sign the bottom. Do it. I'll be back here at midday. You'll get the cash. I'll sign where my signature's required and collect the deeds, and tonight I'll have exchanged a cot in a jail cell for a comfortable bed in my Sheep Mountain property.'

The door clicked open, and he was halfway out into the sweltering heat when he swung back to face the lawyer.

'Just one thing: this has to be legal, all above board – so this is the name I want you to put on those papers.'

FOUR

With his chestnut gelding trotting behind at the end of a short rope, Bodene Rich left Mesquite Flats in the black top-buggy that had carried Bradley Shaw to his death and come to Rich as part of the Sheep Mountain estate. Although he bounced and rattled along the rutted street half expecting Red Booth's brother to open up with a rifle from one of the high windows over the Fat Lady saloon, he made it out of town with his skin intact. Nevertheless, he knew that the fight around George Plant's horse trough had settled nothing and left the two battered hard men with a score to settle. As he headed south towards Sheep Mountain, his eyes were alert for sudden movement in the scorched landscape, or for suspicious flashes of sunlight on metal on the high, rocky ridges.

The trail took him across a white-hot plain bordered by dun hills scarred by fissures, by canyons that cut into the slopes but went nowhere. He had no great distance to travel, but for fear of exhausting the animal in the intense heat he held Shaw's chestnut mare to a steady walk. When a stand of grey-green trees appeared out of the heat haze like dusty sentinels guarding the trail, he pulled the buggy to a halt, stepped down, and walked under the trees to drink deeply from the canteen he had taken from his saddle-bags.

As he sat back against the gnarled bole of one of the trees to smoke a cigarette, the few sparse, dry leaves providing dappled shade but little relief from the merciless sun, he found time to reflect – a luxury that had been impossible during the hours spent in the bare confines of McReady's cell.

Life, he mused, was either jumping up to bite you on the leg, or patting you on the head as it benevolently showered you with bountiful blessings. He'd had his fair share of both in the past twelve months, though the particular blessing he had been seeking had been a long time coming.

At the start of those twelve months he had been forced to leave New York by the sudden death of business partner and friend, Ed Thackray, and ensuing, unanticipated complications that threatened his own life. He had made his way across the continent by rail, stretched his legs in Tucson, Arizona, and gazed towards the hills lying far to the west. Excitement had gripped him like the onset of fever. He had purchased a good horse and rig, and one week later, with the dusty, range-weary appearance of a penniless drifter, had ridden into the far western town of Mesquite Flats. It was a name with a beguiling ring that had been whispered in his ear, in a New York bar, by an Arizona carpetbagger pining for home. Rich had listened to an outpouring of nostalgia, reduced the torrent of praise for the town to a trickle that would approximate the truth, and when he walked his horse down Mesquite Flats' main street he had money in the bank, and a dream.

He wanted a spread out in the hills he had seen from afar, small enough for him and a hired hand to manage easily, but with enough acreage for the successful breeding of palomino horses. He was prepared to wait, and did so, patiently, for six months. At the end of that time, the space he was seeking was given to him, free of charge, but in an unexpected manner. It came in the form of a cell in Yuma Penitentiary. He had been convicted of serious assault, and was looking forward to five years during which he would be scratching for room to breed, not palominos, but roaches or rats.

From the first day, Warden Bradley Shaw believed Rich had been framed, but could do nothing to right the wrong. During the routine interview with the new prisoner, he listened to Rich's story, and Rich noticed a strange light gleaming in his grey eyes. It was at that moment, he had realized, that Shaw, too, had begun to dream – or had seen a dream become a possibility. How Shaw's dream was to affect him, Rich would find out at another time. On that first interview, Shaw merely said that he would love to help Rich find the property he was seeking, but the time he had to serve meant his hands were tied.

All that changed, six months later. A shotgun-toting guard escorted Rich to the warden's office for a second, unexpected interview. The gleam in Shaw's eyes had become a blaze of excitement. Information had come to him, he told Rich, that proved he was innocent. He'd been railroaded, by persons unknown. Accordingly, he was being released immediately, on Shaw's authority.

Not, Shaw admitted with a grin, that he had a single ounce of the authority needed to make such a decision but, as he was resigning his position that very day and they'd be looking for a new warden, he truly didn't give a hoot.

He then showed Rich the letter he had written, and in a comfortable silence they bent over the warden's desk, co-conspirators in an illegal plot to get one man out of jail and help two men realize very different dreams.

And that, Bodene Rich reflected, had been just twenty-four hours ago. For Bradley Shaw, it had all come to nought. His life had been snuffed out by a rifle bullet fired by a bushwhacker who cared nothing for the warden's dreams, or for the dreams of the person for whom he had great affection.

Or was that missing the point, Rich wondered? Was this woman – for clearly it must be a woman – the reason for the killing? If McReady wanted to solve the murder, should he go looking for a marriage that was on the rocks, a woman who was looking for escape, the hard man who would never let her go?

And why, Rich again wondered, should he be pondering the problem, unless – and here his eyes narrowed – this unhappy woman was somehow linked to his own troubles? It was not beyond the bounds of possibility. She knew Bradley Shaw, Shaw had arranged his release. . . .

Rich flicked away his cigarette butt, climbed aboard the top-buggy, sat down on a seat that just about burned the skin off his rear end and pushed on impatiently up the trail. Impatiently, because he had been getting bogged down in pointless cogitation when as yet he had no notion of what he had bought with the hefty wad of money he had handed over in Spencer Hall's office. The warden had mentioned a ranch and stock, but reality could be a couple of sway-backed nags on an acre or so of dusty scrub.

And now Rich grinned ruefully, for again he was letting his imagination run ahead of him and he knew that for six months in Yuma he had been too often alone with his thoughts.

That must change, he vowed – then ducked instinctively as his hat was plucked from his head and the crack of a rifle echoed across the parched scrub.

FIVE

The gunman emerged from behind a rocky outcrop. He was a wiry youngster, no more than twenty, twenty-one, Rich estimated, sitting astride a ragged mustang with flaring nostrils and bright eyes denoting an indomitable spirit. An old Henry rifle was pointed in Rich's direction. The kid's eyes were as bright as the mustang's, and there was a similar wildness in his whole demeanour that warned Rich to keep his hands in sight. Very carefully, he lifted them to shoulder height and sat back.

'That's Bradley Shaw's buggy.'

'It was,' Rich said.

'And now?'

'Now it's mine.'

'But maybe not for much longer,' the kid said, and he grinned. 'You've some explaining to do, and fast. Could save your life.'

'I've been explaining myself since I hit town. To McReady, to Spencer Hall, to Red Booth's brother—'

'Dammit,' the kid blurted, suddenly wide-eyed, 'you're Bodene Rich.'

'More than that,' Rich said, nodding. 'If I've got this figured right, I'm you're new employer.' He paused, slowly lowered his hands. 'You're Shaw's wrangler – right?'

The kid waggled the rifle.

'Matt Danver. Been with him a couple of years. But what the hell d'you mean, you're my new employer?'

'If I can move without getting plugged,' Rich said, 'I'll show you.'

His saddle-bags were by his feet. He bent, dipped his hand inside one of them and brought out a stiff, folded document. He held it up so the white paper was caught in the dazzling sunlight.

'Those are the deeds to the Sheep Mountain spread.'

'BS Connected,' Danver said, staring.

'Part of the explaining I did to Hall was to convince him I had Shaw's permission to buy BS Connected.'

'If you had Shaw's permission,' Danver said, 'why wasn't he there with you in Hall's office.'

'You'd have found out if you'd made it to town. Shaw's dead. He was gunned down yesterday, on his way into Mesquite Flats.'

Danver nodded absently. Rich could see the news hadn't come as a shock. The kid had known something was wrong as soon as he saw Rich driving Shaw's buggy. But now he was trying to work out how the man he thought was doing five years in Yuma could

45

be out of jail and the new owner of BS Connected.

'It's a long story,' Rich offered, 'which we'll no doubt get to later. But right now I want to know if I'm going to be raising palominos in a dust bowl, or on something resembling the meadows I'm used to back East.'

He slipped two bits of information into the short speech, saw Danver pick them up, and knew for a wrangler the mention of palominos would have been like dangling a carrot in front of a donkey's nose.

'So unless you had important business in town,' Rich said, smiling, 'why don't you turn that nag around and lead the way so I can inspect my new home?'

'Nag!' Danver said scornfully. Then, slipping the rifle into its boot, he spun the mustang on a dime and set off down the trail at a fast gallop.

Rich followed at what he intended to be a slower pace. But the mare had recognized Danver and, in what had to be a tribute to the wrangler's humane handling of the horses in his care, she didn't want to be left behind. She was kicking up her heels, tossing her head and looking back at Rich, who laughed for the first time since he'd walked out of Yuma, relented and slackened the reins. They sped down the trail at a rollicking pace, eating the kid's billowing dust, not catching him but somehow managing to keep him in sight.

In such a manner they rounded a sweeping bend and Rich saw before him an ugly, low-slung, single-storey ranch house. His first sight of his purchase –

and he was not impressed. Knock it down, rebuild, he thought. Easy enough to do when cash was available, and he had plenty.

The house was set at the top of a gentle slope of rich blue grass that Shaw must have imported, probably from Kentucky, and somehow managed to irrigate. Not too difficult, Rich decided after a moment's thought, for he realized that Flats Creek, which had figured in Dieter Bauer's dispute with Red Booth, must flow between BS Connected and the Bauer spread. Behind the house the ground sloped more steeply, and beyond that a rock ridge was partly hidden by a stand of dark pines outlined against the white-hot skies.

When he brought his gaze back to the level ground, he saw that Danver had pulled his bronc to a halt in the drive leading up to the house and was talking to a woman on a piebald pony.

Even from a distance, and seated on a horse, she looked graceful, elegant. *And, damn me,* Rich thought as he drew nearer, *she should do, too, because if that isn't Ellie Bauer then I'll eat my hat.*

'You realize you're the talk of the town?' Ellie Bauer said.

They'd moved to the shaded gallery fronting the house, and were sitting on wooden chairs that looked as old as Bradley Shaw. Young Danver had taken charge of the mare and Rich's chestnut gelding and, with a pail of water, cloths, and boundless energy, was rubbing them both down outside the barn next to the corral. Rich had cast a glance in that direction, and figured that if the four horses with their heads over the corral's top rail were all the stock Shaw had, then he'd been dreaming of a getaway for some time. And, with Ellie Bauer showing up the day after he died, it didn't take a Pinkertons' agent to figure out who had been the object of his affections.

'I've been the talk of the town,' Rich said, 'since the day I rode in. Not too many New Yorkers pass this way. Not many who do end up in the Yuma Pen.'

'For a crime they didn't commit,' Ellie Bauer said softly.

She wore a dark split skirt, a white blouse. Her dark hair hung loose. A flat-crowned black hat rested in her lap.

'Is that your opinion, or something you know for a fact?'

An expression that was a cross between a smile and a thoughtful pout crossed her face.

'You're sitting here a free man, Mr Rich. And I'm very pleased, more pleased, perhaps, than you will ever know.'

'Oh? And why would that be?'

'There was a decision I thought I might have to make. Your release means it may no longer be necessary. . . .' She hesitated, seemed about to say more, then smiled. 'Anyway, that's enough about my problems. I said you were imprisoned for a crime you did not commit. You're here now, free to do as you please, and that suggests the authorities realized their mistake.'

48

'Bradley Shaw took it upon himself to unlock the gates and set me loose,' Rich said. 'He told me he had information that proved I'd been framed. Didn't tell me where it came from. He admitted he did not have the authority to release me, but didn't give a damn because he was resigning that very day.'

'Really,' Ellie Bauer said, her dark eyes wide as if in surprise, but sparkling with amusement.

'In the letter he gave to me to show to Spencer Hall, he spelled out why he was leaving Yuma.' Rich paused, watched Ellie Bauer. 'You got any ideas on that?'

'Isn't that a rather impertinent question?'

'You're here. Your spread's on the other side of the creek, you must have known Shaw. Talked to him. Listened to an old man's dreams.'

'Not so old.' She smiled, but now there was sadness in her eyes. Then she shook her head. 'I'm a married woman, Mr Rich. Brad and I were good friends, and if you'd heard rumours to suggest otherwise, they are wrong. My son went to school with Matt Danver. I heard what had happened to Brad, I came here to offer Matt a job.'

It was Rich's turn to smile, but his was cynical.

'You really think Danver would have worked under Al Ferris? Or for your husband?'

'Perhaps not, but it no longer matters, does it?' she said. 'Another reason you're the talk of the town is because you're the new owner of BS Connected. You intend to breed palominos. There's a rumour that you have more than enough money to do that,

49

so Matt's position here as wrangler would appear to be secure.'

Rich's chair creaked as he leaned back, stretched his legs. Ellie Bauer had given away no secrets, had held on to her composure even when the conversation had circled around the death of Bradley Shaw. She was clearly an intelligent woman, and expressed herself with a clarity Rich admired. Because of that, her last words troubled him, and his unease was increased because she was watching and waiting with patient expectancy.

'All right, I'll bite,' he said softly. 'What exactly do you mean by appears to be secure?'

'There were two strangers in town. A strange pair. Not westerners. One was about Brad's age, the other much younger. They were talking to Spencer Hall when I came out of the bank.'

'And?'

'I couldn't help overhearing. They were asking about you. Bodene Rich. They knew you'd been released from Yuma. They wanted to know if you'd returned to Mesquite Flats and, if so, where they could find you.'

SIX

Edward Thackray and his son, Erskine, had listened to the Mesquite Spring's lawyer's information without surprise. Hell, they knew damn well the man they were hunting had cash, and if he figured he was safe then why wouldn't he start to splash it around? Especially, Edward pointed out, when he was fresh out of a cell he'd expected to occupy for the next five years.

It was midday. They were in Millie's café, drinking black coffee and casting occasional glances at the jail across the street.

'The fact that he's bought property tells me he believes he's in the clear. He's got no worries, and he's not going anywhere in a hurry,' Edward said. 'That tells me we can spend the day resting up without fear of him hightailing, and leave the biggest surprise of this Bodene Rich's life until tomorrow.'

'Risky. If he gets word we're here, that could be too late.'

'Who's going to tell him? You?'

'Damn right I am,' Erskine said, grinning. 'But I'll do it when we're face to face, and over the barrel of a gun.'

'Before that,' his father said, 'we'll have a talk with the town marshal, see what we can learn. A man short on facts is a man short of ammunition – but that, too, can be dealt with first thing tomorrow. Right now my only interest is in that hotel we passed. I'd like to think they've got soft feather beds, but expect something less salubrious. Never mind. Lay me in whatever they've got, take off my boots, and I'll sleep the goddamn clock around.'

Dan McReady had his feet up on the desk and was idly discussing Bodene Rich with his son, Pete, when the two strangers walked into his office the next morning. He'd watched them ride into town, had learned from Spencer Hall that they had been enquiring about Rich, and was at once intrigued. It had taken but one casual glance to tell him the two men were city slickers, most likely from back East. Bodene Rich was from New York, and if the two strangers had followed him all the way across a continent, their interest in him had to be serious. It was unlikely they were bringing good news. Good news was almost always about money, and Rich was already prosperous. McReady found himself wondering yet again where the man had got his cash.

'I'm Ed Thackray,' the grey haired man said, doffing an expensive Stetson hat and sinking onto a hard chair. 'My boy, Erskine.' He gestured, mopped his brow. 'We've walked across from the hotel. Is it always this hot this early?'

'Not always.' McReady grinned. 'Midsummer gets hotter.' He rocked gently in his chair. 'You've come about Bodene Rich.'

'To the right place, by the sound of it; you're a sharp one.'

'Not too hard to work out. Saw you talking to Spencer Hall. Spencer had dealings with Rich yesterday, and the whole town's not stopped talking.' McReady raised an eyebrow. 'Are you about to add to his troubles?'

'Maybe. Then again, maybe not.'

'Meaning?'

'A man bought BS Connected. What name did that lawyer put on the papers?'

'Bodene Rich,' Pete McReady said. 'Who else?' The deputy's badge on his vest caught the sun as he half-turned to look at his father, then back at Thackray. 'If there is some doubt about a name written on paper, Spencer Hall is the man to ask.'

'What name did you have in mind?' Dan McReady said.

'Dean Rickard,' Ed Thackray said softly.

'The man who used a .45 revolver to plug my brother in the back,' Erskine Thackray said, 'and walked away with a fortune, half of which is rightfully ours.'

The office door was wide open, the noise of the bustling small Arizona town drifting in on the haze of dust. Ed Thackray was doing most of the talking.

'Rickard was in partnership with my elder son, named Edward after me and his grandad,' he said. 'Ed and Rickard sold cheap accident- and life-insurance to New York businesses. Hawked it around the streets, had a coupla girls working in a shabby office; made a lot of money. Then some eighteen months ago, middle of the night, Ed was shot down in cold blood. The next day Rickard went missing. We checked with the bank. They wouldn't give details, but did tell us the business account was empty.' His grin was cold. 'Erskine and me, we put two and two together. That was the day we started hunting.'

'Might have been empty for some time, a business on the rocks. Rickard could have been murdered by commercial rivals, an irate husband, his body dumped in the river,' McReady said.

'A dead man doesn't clear his apartment,' Erskine said. 'A dead man doesn't buy a train ticket out of New York.'

'A ticket to where?'

'Doesn't matter,' Thackray said. 'The trail went dead, so we called in the Pinkertons. Took 'em six months to find him.'

'If it's him.'

'It's him. Dean Rickard. Bodene Rich. Put those two together and someone as sharp as you are can see he tried to be too clever, and getting slammed into Yuma was his bad luck, our good fortune. It gave him away. The Pinkertons had feelers out, and they were looking at newspapers. There was an inch in the

Yuma weekly about a man who'd been convicted of assault. Pinkertons liked the bit that said he was a New Yorker who'd arrived in Mesquite Flats six months previous.'

'Yeah, and it was six months ago he was locked up,' McReady said. 'What took you so long?'

'A man in jail's going nowhere. The accommodation is less than basic, the tenants fearsome. We let him sweat, maybe pick up a few bruises, broken bones.'

'And now?'

'We have another talk with the lawyer. Make sure. And when we are sure—'

'Matt Danver's across at the livery,' Pete McReady said.

He'd been half-listening, smoking a cigarette as he idly watched the street's activity. Now he got up and crossed the office to step out onto the sunlit plank walk.

'Looks like he's handing a couple of Shaw's thoroughbreds to George.' He looked over his shoulder. 'Now, why would he do that? Rich bought the spread. Common sense tells me he'd keep Matt on as wrangler. So why move the horses?'

'Take a walk across,' McReady said, 'ask George what's going on.'

Thackray was watching McReady. As Pete stepped down into the dust and began threading his way between trundling wagons, lathered horses and sweating riders, he cleared his throat.

'Is there a reason for sending your deputy? You got

some preconceived notions on that situation?'

'Not especially. Rich leans towards palominos. And if those two are poor stock, well, that's as good a reason as any for putting them up for sale.'

His eyes showed clearly that was not what he believed. He shrugged, looked keenly at Thackray. 'You've got Rich down for your son's murder. Does that fit with what you know about the man? Rich? He got a history of violent behaviour?'

'He's no powder puff, for sure,' Ed Thackray said. 'Some of the bars in the big city cater to a tough clientèle. Rich frequented them, never looked out of place. I hear he had a dust up that alerted the police.'

'You're digging,' Erskine Thackray said perceptively. 'We went first to the Yuma pen, following the newspaper lead, found out he'd been released early. That throws doubt on the original conviction. As marshal, you would have been involved. His early release reflects badly on you. If you arrested him, you're looking for justification, or something in his character that says you were more likely right than wrong.'

'I'm more interested in you two. Most people in Mesquite Flats are law abiding citizens. When Bodene Rich broke Red Booth's legs with an iron bar, the mood in town turned ugly. It was somewhat appeased when he got sent to the pen, but now he's back, and his early release has already stirred up trouble.'

Ed Thackray was grinning slyly.

'And that creates a problem. The ex-con is now a wealthy landowner, and, as such, is contributing to your pay packet. Makes running him out of town for the public good a mite difficult, not to say unappealing. Then, one early morning you're sitting scratching your head and we walk in the door. You've listened to our story; you know why we're here; you don't know what we intend to do.'

'I know you're not heading out to the BS Connected to shake Bodene Rich by the hand.'

'So you can see a glimmer of light. The alternative to a handshake is something you won't put into words, so I'll do it for you: it's called an eye for an eye. That gets Rich out of your hair and, with him consigned to history, Mesquite Flats quits seething like a pot on red-hot coals and goes back to basking lazily in the sun.'

'As for the relieved town marshal,' Erskine said softly, persuasively, 'he yawns, sits back with his feet on his desk and watches the world go by.'

There was a long silence. Flies buzzed against the window. A wagon rattled, a teamster yelled hoarsely and cracked his whip.

'If you're asking for my approval,' McReady said at last, 'you won't get it: as an officer of the law, I cannot condone violence.'

But the Thackrays were already up on their feet and heading for the door.

'Approval is not something high on our list of wants,' Ed Thackray said. 'Right now we're heading across the street to the general store to make a couple of purchases. One of 'em might seem to you a little unusual, but if you get wind of it I'd suggest you ponder for a while, go in whichever direction your mind takes you to reach a conclusion – then keep your mouth tight shut.'

And, tipping his hat, and smiling without a hint of menace, Ed Thackray followed his son out into the dust and the heat of Mesquite Flats' main street.

SEVEN

It was dusk when Bodene Rich and Matt Danver mounted their horses and set them to the slope leading to the pines and the rocky ridge. The two horses whickered at them from the end corral as they rode by. Away from the ranch house they left behind them the rich blue grass, their horses' hoofs rattling on the harder ground. A coyote's cry came to them mournfully out of the rising mists. A bird, as black as night, was a dark shadow passing overhead with a whisper of sound as it swooped towards the distant creek.

They rode without speaking, letting the horses pick their way across the rough, stony ground. The gentle slope quickly turned into a steep climb, then levelled as the horses moved onto soft pine needles at the edge of the trees that were like a dark wall halting their progress.

Danver broke the silence.

'Here? Or further on?'

'You're the local,' Rich said. 'I want to be close enough to see, but not close enough to be seen too easily. The ridge could be too far – but it's your call.'

'With a rifle, nothing's too far.' Danver grinned. 'OK, I say we push on. Staying here, we're so close we'd need to move deep into the trees. Up on the ridge we'll be out in the open with a clear view, but behind rocks – and if they're interested in the house they won't lift their gaze that high.'

Rich grunted his agreement. Danver continued to lead the way. They skirted the pines and found a winding track that took them away from the trees and onto an escarpment where loose scree made footing treacherous. The horses snorted their disapproval and began climbing jerkily. Danver, young but an experienced wrangler, swung out of the saddle. Rich followed suit, and both men struggled upwards alongside the horses, hanging on to the saddle-horns as sharp rocks rolled beneath their boots. Then, abruptly, they reached a level shelf. Horses and men stopped to catch their breath. Rich glanced back, and saw that already they could look down across the tops of the pines to the back of the house.

'We nearly there?'

'See for yourself.'

Danver swung an arm. The track curled away into a wide crack in the rock face. The rimrock was no more than fifty feet above them, a jagged line painted a warm pink by the last rays of the sun sinking behind hills far to the west.

It was also deceptive. Rich had been expecting the land on the far side of the rimrock to drop steeply. Instead, when they emerged from the fault in the rock face and ground-tethered the horses, he found himself on coarse dry grass covering a plateau that sloped easily away into the distance.

'From here,' Matt Danver said, 'a man with a rifle is always in control, and cannot be dislodged. If he commences shooting, the only thing a target any-where near the house can do is run for it.'

'Which is what your former employer was unable to do,' Rich said. 'The only shot fired was by a man settled on a ridge probably much like this one. It took Bradley Shaw's life, put an end to Ellie Bauer's dreams of escape.'

Yards away, peering down from the jagged rocks at the distant ranch house and the Mesquite Flats trail, Danver flicked a glance backwards.

'You've got it all figured, haven't you?'

'Don't need to be a professor to do that. Shaw had given up his job and was planning on heading east with a companion. And who was waiting here when we rode in? Ellie Bauer.' Rich smiled grimly in the gloom. 'Kris Bauer's what, nineteen? I was here six months before I got locked up, more than enough time to have that son of a bitch Dieter Bauer all weighed up. Ellie, still young, still beautiful, had been enduring life with a monster for twenty years.'

They'd moved away from BS Connected land and up onto the high ridge because Bodene Rich didn't expect the Thackrays to waste any time. They'd found him; they'd kill him; they'd head home. His only other option had been to remain in the house and confront them head on, but that would have been too risky.

By midday they'd already meticulously planned their move to high ground.

It had been Danver's idea to take two of the four horses remaining from Bradley Shaw's stock into town and stable them with George Plant. They intended climbing up to the ridge on horseback because Danver flatly refused to walk, and he'd pointed out that leaving themselves afoot would be plain foolish. Two unsaddled horses in the corral, Danver went on, would lead the Thackrays to believe that Rich was asleep in the ranch house, Danver in the small bunkhouse.

To add weight to the deception, Rich decided to leave oil lamps lit, but well back from any windows so the Thackrays would see little until they were close in. And they would come in close because . . . well, at that point Rich left it. The whole idea of going up to the ridge was to watch and wait. What happened after that, what they were forced to do after that, was dependent on the Thackrays' intentions and subsequent actions.

The news Danver brought back with him from

Mesquite Flats had convinced Rich that he had been right to move out of the house. His concern had been that the Thackrays would enlist help, and that now appeared likely. Danver had seen father and son talking to McReady over at the jail, and Rich knew that Ed Thackray was a persuasive talker. Later, when leaving town, Danver had ridden past Queenie's Fat Lady saloon and seen the two Easterners talking to Frank Booth.

McReady, hanging on to his job as town marshal, would listen but do nothing. But in Frank Booth, the Thackrays would have found a man more than willing to ride with them, more than willing to do anything it took to avenge the assault that had left his brother a cripple.

Rich and Danver had moved to the edge of the high ground where naked rocks on the rim rose high to afford cover yet gave then a clear view if they moved a short pace right or left. For the past few hours – broken by the occasional brisk walk to keep muscles flexible – they had been sitting on the coarse grass with their backs to the rough rock.

It was approaching midnight. The air was chill, the skies were luminous but there was no moon, and mist spreading in all directions from Flats Creek made it almost impossible to see the ranch house.

A little way down the gentle slope the two horses dozed, vapour drifting from their nostrils. Matt Danver was smoking, cupping the glowing cigarette in his hand – though there was little chance of it being seen from their position. Rich had his legs stretched out, his Stetson tipped over his face. He was trying to stay awake.

Suddenly he sat up straight.

'Listen,' he said.

They were high above the house. Sound travels well on clear night air, but their position made any source difficult to pin down. Rich thought he had heard the faint ring of metal on stone. The two men waited. It came again, a musical sound filled with menace. Then a horse snorted.

Rich spun, poked his head around the sheltering rock, looked down at the dark serrated outline of the pines and tried to see over and beyond them. Danver was doing the same, and cursing softly.

'Too misty. Can see as far as the back of the house – just.'

'But I was right. I can hear horses clearly now. Riders are approaching along the trail from town.'

'Two of 'em,' Danver said after a moment. 'If it's your friends from back East, they're doing this on their own. No local guns.'

'This being?'

Danver chuckled. 'Well, we're up here, they're down there. Whatever they've got planned they sure as hell can't plug you, so your guess is as good as mine.'

'Wait and watch was the idea – but we might as well be wearing blindfolds.'

'So what then? Move down closer?'

'We get careless it could give the game away.'

'Worth a try. Lamps lit in the house, horses in the corral. If they hear something, the rattle of stone, they'll blame foxes, coyotes.'

Rich rolled, came to his feet.

'Let's go. And this time we'll walk.'

They jogged towards ground that became bare of grass and dropped sharply into the cleft in the rock face where they had ridden. Going down on foot it was much easier to keep quiet. The rock walls closed in on them as they scrambled down the crevice. For the short time it took to descend, all sound was cut off. When the emerged into the open air they again caught the rattle of hoofs, already much closer to the house – and now Rich and Danver were approaching the treacherous loose scree above the pines.

'Go round,' Danver said softly, pointing to his right.

The scree was flanked by slopes carpeted with soft grass. They cut along the top edge of the loose rock escarpment, walking awkwardly across the steep incline. Because they were closer to the pines, their view down to the mist-shrouded ranch house was blocked. Impatiently, Rich jogged past Danver, reached the grass and turned downhill. It was damp. He slipped, regained his footing, made it down to the stand of trees at a stumbling run. This time, on foot, he saved time by going straight through the timber, grimacing in the pine-scented darkness as dead twigs crackled beneath his feet.

When he broke through the edge of the trees he was on the patch of level ground, treading on soft pine needles. He paused to take a breath. Danver caught up with him. Rich held him back with an out-stretched arm.

'They'll not see us against the trees,' Rich said. 'But this close, we can see through the mist.'

'Watch and wait,' Danver said, echoing Rich's words. 'And it looks like that won't be too long.'

Squinting across the ranch-house's shingle roof, he dropped his hand to his holster and loosened his six-gun.

The two men from New York were out of the saddle and walking across the stretch of blue grass fronting the house. The river mist blurred the scene so that everything was seen through a white haze, but Bodene Rich had no difficulty recognizing his former business partner's relatives. Ed Thackray was leading the way, treading carefully, looking to right and left. He was followed by the taller figure of his son, Erskine.

'They're acting cautious,' Matt Danver said. 'They've seen the lamps, seen the horses, figure we're both asleep. But . . . we'll lose sight of them when they get close to the house.' He glanced side-ways, frowning at Rich. 'You going to stand here, let them break in.'

Rich was squinting into the mist, watching Erskine Thackray.

'What's he carrying? The big feller?'

'I . . . don't know. Looks like. . . .' Danver cursed. 'Gone,' he said, as the two men disappeared from sight, 'but if I was asked to guess I'd say it was—'

'A small drum,' Rich finished for him. 'Probably full of kerosene. They're going to set fire to the house, burn me out.'

'Then let's go, let's stop those sons of—'

'No.'

Rich grabbed the younger man's arm as he started forward.

'Hell,' Danver swore, 'you going to let them do that?'

'Keep your voice down.'

Rich was holding tight to Danver's arm, and listening. The young man shook him off, but stayed where he was. He was eyeing Rich with disgust, then casting quick glances towards the house. They could hear low voices; then liquid splashing. Danver spread his hands, slapped his thighs, began to pace angrily to and fro on the pine needles.

Then, unmistakably, they could smell burning kerosene. Seconds later they heard crackling, and the smell of burning wood was added to the hot reek of flaming oil.

'If I'm dead,' Rich said softly, 'a lot of guilty folk in these parts will drop their guard.'

'That's you,' Danver said, catching on at once. 'But unless they burn down the bunkhouse, I'm alive to tell the tale.'

'Even better. You saw everything, tried to break into the burning building but were driven back by the heat.' Rich grinned. 'Come on, I think it's time we returned to the horses.'

And, as the cold river mist began to be warmed by

the glow from the fire and the two Thackrays beat a hasty retreat, Rich turned away from the doomed ranch house and started back through the pine woods.

EIGHT

It was just after eight the next morning, and Marshal Dan McReady was on the plank walk outside the general store when Ed and Erskine Thackray came riding down the main street. He watched the two Easterners cut across to the livery barn and ride straight inside, followed them on foot at a leisurely pace – nodding and smiling affably to passers by – and stopped next to the horse trough and rickety windmill to roll a cigarette.

The smoke fixed and lit, McReady leaned back against the windmill's warped timber framework and found himself marvelling at the strange ways of folk brought up in the big city. After what he'd learned from his talk with Wilson over at the general store, he was pretty sure he knew what the Thackrays had been up to. If he'd got it right, he couldn't comprehend what they were doing in town.

He stood enjoying his smoke for a good ten minutes. Then Ed Thackray and his son came walking bold as brass out of the livery barn, and turned towards Millie's café. Thackray senior glanced casually about him as he headed up the street, caught sight of McReady and did a swift double take. He stopped, said something out of the corner of his mouth. Then both men turned on their heels and came walking over.

McReady flicked away his half-smoked cigarette.

'Glad we caught you, Marshal,' Ed Thackray said. 'I'm afraid we have tragic news.'

'Can't be that bad,' McReady said, 'if you can waste ten minutes talking to George Plant then start thinking about filling your bellies.'

'Unfortunately, wasting minutes or hours before reporting it to you makes not a scrap of difference,' Thackray said. 'Bodene Rich is dead. He died in a fire that completely destroyed his house out at Sheep Mountain.'

'Bodene Rich, or Dean Rickard?'

'Sadly, that's something we will never know for sure,' Thackray said. 'I had it fixed in my mind that Rich was the man we were looking for, and I was going to put the question to him. We were too late, and as there's a limit to the time we can spend hunting down my son's killer, that's something we will have to live with.'

'Did you try to save him?'

'We're not without heart, Marshal. Rich, Rickard, was a human being, and we did what we could. But when we arrived at the scene the fire had taken hold, and we were beaten back by the fierce heat.'

McReady nodded absently. He was gazing up the

street, still trying to comprehend the Thackrays' thinking, wondering now if they took all small-town lawmen to be complete idiots.

'What did you do with the oil drum?' he said softly.

The question sliced through the hot air, cut cleanly through the Thackrays' smug confidence. Ed Thackray shifted his feet in the dust.

'What oil drum?'

'The one you got Wilson over at the general store to fill with kerosene. The one your son lashed behind his saddle and carried out of town.'

'I'm not sure—'

'Hell, last time you were here you as good as told me what you were doing, warned me to keep my mouth shut.'

'No, you've got the wrong end of the stick—'

'What did you do?' McReady went on relentlessly. 'Make damn sure Rich was sleeping, then splash kerosene over the walls and strike a match? And did you then burn down the bunkhouse? And if you didn't, d'you realize that was a bad mistake, because Matt Danver the wrangler sleeps there and, if I know Matt, he'll have seen everything?'

'Jesus Christ,' Erskine Thackray said thickly.

'Yeah, well, right now he's the only one can help you,' Dan McReady said, and he drew his six-gun and cocked it with a metallic snap. 'Hoist your hands, both of you, and walk ahead of me over to the jail. I'm arresting the two of you for the cold-blooded murder of Bodene Rich.'

*

It was late afternoon when Al Ferris got back to the Bauer spread. He had been in town picking up supplies, and had moved on to the Fat Lady to slake his thirst. There, rather than listen to gossip, he had moved to the end of the bar to drink sullenly while brooding on the situation at the ranch where he was foreman. When he returned to the spread on Flats Creek, the buckboard only half laden, Bauer had blown his top.

'What the hell's going on, Ferris? What's Wilson playing at?'

'The bill you're running up,' Ferris countered, 'you're lucky I didn't return empty. Which I likely will, next time. And if you want to know what Wilson's playing at, he's giving you a flat ultimatum: no more credit, clear the account by the end of the month. Until then it's cash on the nail or you get nothing.'

Bauer turned and walked away, his face red, his mouth working.

'Unload, then get back to work,' he called over his shoulder.

'Doing what? You've run down the stock, the hands are sitting chewing tobacco and whittling while they wait for last month's pay. . . .'

Bauer blanked him out.

He stormed into the house, slammed the door behind him, and glared at his son.

'Nothing to do?'

'I was listening, I heard Al, and you know he's right. This place is finished—'

He broke off as a vicious backhand blow almost knocked him off the hard chair. Blood trickled down his chin. He glared at Dieter, his eyes hot.

'Where's your ma?'

'What?'

'For Christ's sake, your ma – you got any idea where she is? I haven't seen her since yesterday. She went out late morning, didn't come home.'

'I don't know.'

'You sure?'

'Of course I'm sure. Anyway, if she's got any sense—'

He saw his father's fists clench, stopped, mumbled something inaudible then fumbled for his bandanna and covered his bloody mouth.

'Then here's another one for you,' Dieter said. 'And I want the truth. I've never come straight out and asked you, but I'm doing it now. Did you go down to the creek twelve months ago and use an iron bar on Red Booth?'

'You didn't ask me, but I told you—'

'I'm askin' now, so tell me again: was it you turned Red Booth into a cripple?'

'Why?'

Dieter had been heading for the whiskey bottle. Now he swung round.

'Because Bodene Rich being back in town changes everything, and the circumstances of his return could work in our favour. Whenever a man dies, suddenly the whole world starts remembering his good points, every mean bastard becomes a philan-

thropist, every sinner a saint. Yesterday Bradley Shaw
was murdered. He wasn't well liked, maybe not even
known all that well, but now every man in town will
claim he was his friend.'

'Get to the point.'

'I will. But I need an answer.'

'I'm clear,' Kris Bauer said, dabbing his lip. 'The
night Booth got his legs broke I was nowhere near
the creek.'

'Your ma's been hinting at the exact opposite.
There's no telling who's been listening to her.'

'The one man she was closest to,' Kris said, treading carefully, 'is the one who got hisself killed.'

'Nevertheless, there's always been people who,
from they day he was convicted, have been uncertain
about Bodene Rich's guilt,' Dieter Bauer said.
'Which brings me to the point I was about to make.'

He'd reached the whiskey bottle, and now he
splashed liquor into a glass and knocked back half of
it without taking his eyes off his son.

'Don't worry your head over new evidence that got
Rich released,' he said. 'My guess is you're right, and
it's buried six feet deep with Bradley Shaw. The point
is he was put there by an unknown gunman. You
were in town yesterday. Who rode in a couple of
hours after Shaw bit the dust?'

'Bodene Rich,' Kris said.

'A man convicted of a brutal assault, but mysteri-
ously out of jail. Hours after his release, the prison
warden is in his top-buggy on a deserted road, and
he's shot dead. Just like that.' He flicked his now

empty glass with a fingernail, the sharp ring startling Kris. Dieter grinned. 'You following this? You see the point I'm making?'

And now there was the gleam of dawning understanding in Kris Bauer's eyes.

'Just like McReady did when Rich rode in, everyone in Mesquite Flats will blame the jailbird,' he said, feeling his way, picking his words as he watched his father. Seeing his nod, he went on, 'And because Shaw's dead, suddenly the old prison warden was everybody's friend. He's been bushwhacked, they'll take it personally, and they'll be angry.'

'Sure they'll be angry,' Dieter said. 'But they'll know that anger's not enough, they'll know they should act to put things right, they should do something. Trouble is,' Dieter said softly, 'they're mostly law abiding citizens, and law abiding citizens don't go out and hang a man from the nearest tree just because they're riled. People like that need proof.'

'Yeah, but if the proof died with Bradley Shaw—'

'I'm talking about proof that Bodene Rich is rotten to the core. You see what I'm getting at? That makes it easy. If it's proof they need, proof that Rich is a bad apple then, hell, there's one sure-fire way of giving it to them.'

Dieter Bauer grinned wickedly. The cork popped as he jerked it out of the bottle. Whiskey splashed into the glass. He tossed back the raw spirit, poured another measure, and handed this full glass to his son.

'Drink that down, then go get Al. If the town's

sitting on the fence and not sure which way to jump, by tomorrow morning they'll have the answer.'

NINE

'You were wrong to try,' Red Booth said. 'Wrong to involve those two no-good drifters, wrong to risk getting yourself bad hurt.'

'Bodene Rich has been set free, my brother's a cripple—'

'Don't say that.'

The reprimand was delivered harshly, and was followed by a strained silence in which could be heard the measured ticking of an old clock, the click of hot iron.

It was late evening. The two brothers were sitting in the cramped living-room of their house close to Flats Creek. The light came from a single oil lamp. Since the attack six months ago they had exercised extreme caution. Both men knew that low light didn't tell trespassers that there was nobody at home, but somehow it made the Booths more comfortable to know that they were not blatantly advertising their presence. The man who had attacked Red may, until yesterday, have been safely behind bars, but the greater danger had always come from their defiance of Dieter Bauer.

'My legs were broken,' Red Booth said, as if explanation were needed. 'I walk with a limp. I'm rarely free from pain. But it doesn't stop me working, doesn't stop me doing my fair share.'

'I'm sorry.'

Frank Booth's right eye was a thin slit in a shiny purple swelling. He was standing by the glowing iron stove. Metal clattered as he poured coffee. He handed a cup to his brother, touched him on the shoulder. When he sat down, his battered face was a picture of frustration.

Red Booth grinned, lifting the gloom.

'Your heart will give out, Frank. Stop wasting your energy on what cannot be changed. You paid two men to help you take your anger out on Bodene Rich, but that would have been a second wrong, and you know what they say.'

'It would have been right in my eyes. You argued with him outside the Fat Lady. You insulted him by calling him a work-shy drifter, but what he did that night – attacking you from behind – was an extreme reaction, out of all proportion, the actions of a coward. Seeing him pay for what he did would have given me some peace.'

'No. You'd have been tormented by guilt.'

'Mebbe so, but the satisfaction would have been worth the price. Coming on top of the other troubles, the attack. . . .' He spread his hands helplessly. 'We came here full of fight, Red, but Bauer's won, defeat is staring us in the face.'

'Leaving here,' Red Booth said, 'is not defeat. Sensible armies retreat when facing overwhelming odds. Look on it as a tactical withdrawal. We move on to richer pastures, make a fresh start.'

'And your mind's set on this?'

'Mine and yours; we discussed it at length, finally reached agreement; Bauer's kept quiet, but that won't last because, whatever we say, this is his land.' He shrugged. 'We agreed, then Bodene Rich returned and you were distracted. But we don't change good plans so you can get even.'

Frank Booth spent time rolling a cigarette. When he struck a match and sucked in the harsh smoke, his one good eye was thoughtful.

'I'd be a whole lot happier,' he said quietly, 'if I could leave here knowing we'd put the blame in its rightful place. You talked about torment, and what's tormenting me is that maybe I went after the wrong man. OK, when we ganged up on him outside Plant's barn it failed anyway and single-handed he bested the three of us. But if I was wrong, if *you and me* were wrong and it wasn't Rich attacked you, then—'

But Red was no longer listening. He was half out of his chair, his eyes on the door. Suddenly Frank caught the sounds that had warned his brother. He made a lunge for the wall, were a shotgun rested lengthwise on wooden pegs.

He was too late.

The was kicked open. Three men piled into the small, hot room. They had coarse linen bags over their heads, with slits through which could be seen the glint of cold eyes. Two drawn six-guns caught the lamplight. The third man was carrying a wooden stave.

Dust came in with them, the dry dust of a warm Arizona night, but above that could be detected the reek of male sweat. It was the stink of hard men intent on violence.

'We're leaving,' Frank Booth said hastily. 'No need to do this, by tomorrow—'

One of the men carrying six-guns pounced. He came in from Frank's blind side, flung a strong arm around his throat from behind and dragged him off his feet. The man with the stave crossed the room in three long strides. Red Booth was out of his chair, but he was slowed by his weakened legs. He saw his attacker coming, flung the remains of his coffee in his face. Then the heavy wooden stave was whipped around in a vicious horizontal swing. It caught Red Booth behind the ear. His eyes rolled. He hit the earth floor with a thump and lay still.

The man holding Frank laughed harshly.

'You're getting real good at that, Bodene,' he said. 'Now let's see what you can do with this one.'

Frank Booth kicked helplessly. His boots met thin air. The arm around his throat was choking him. A hand had hold of his belt. Still struggling, he was wrestled out through the door. His head cracked against the jamb. Through blurred eyes he saw the pale gleam of a high moon behind thin clouds, three horses like ghosts seen through the hanging mists drifting in from the placid waters of Flats Creek.

Then, abruptly, he was released. He staggered forward weakly. Scattered thoughts raced indecisively. He was torn between charging back into the house to help his brother, or turning and fighting. Instead, he sucked in air and did what he knew was sensible: he turned to run.

He ran straight into the swinging wooden stave. It struck him like an axe, an inch above his swollen left eyebrow, and it was as if someone had blown out the flame of their single oil lamp and the light from that, and the pale floating moon, had suddenly been extinguished.

TEN

'Give that to me again,' Dan McReady said, 'because I'm damned if I can make sense of it.'

He was leaning against the wall outside the jail, soaking up the hot sun. His son Pete was in the doorway, smoking. They were both looking idly across at the livery barn where Mesquite Flats' second deputy was talking to George Plant about a night-time intruder.

'I talked to several people at the Yuma Penitentiary. I discovered that Bradley Shaw told a colleague he had evidence proving Bodene Rich had been wrongly imprisoned.'

'Right. But Shaw didn't give details.'

'No. This colleague pressed him for more information, but got nowhere. He politely suggested to Shaw that by releasing Rich the warden was putting his job on the line. Shaw kept his mouth shut, grinned sort of secretively, and that was that.'

'Not quite. What was it this colleague said? Shaw told him he would be putting all relevant details, including the guilty man's name, into a letter?'

'Yes.'

'But why would Shaw send a letter to his place of work? What does that suggest?'

'Shaw was finished. When he left Yuma that day, he had no intention of ever going back to the prison.'

'Which is neither here nor there, but is still mighty interesting,' McReady said softly. 'Dammit, he had a name, kept it to himself, then got bushwhacked before he could put anything in writing.'

'But the information he had must have come from somewhere, from someone. Someone out there knows who attacked Red Booth. And that someone has to be here in Mesquite Flats.'

'Yeah.'

Dan McReady nodded, watched a loaded buckboard trundle by in a cloud of dust, spat within inches of basking lizard.

'What was it Rich said when he rode into town the day Shaw was plugged?'

Pete flicked his cigarette into the street.

'He told us to look at Al Ferris for the attack on Red Booth.'

'Ferris works for Dieter Bauer, and that was the point Rich was making. But talking to Bauer would be a waste of time.'

'Same goes for his son, Kris. But there is one person at the Bauer spread blessed with some intelligence.'

'Ellie Bauer; and it's no secret that married woman was pretty thick with Warden Bradley Shaw,'

McReady said, and he pushed away from the wall.
'You'd best go out there and talk to her.'

'Had to be Matt Danver,' McReady said, frowning
and licking a pencil.

His second deputy, a middle-aged man called
Brown, had just told him that the livery barn had
been broken into, but nothing stolen. Instead, the
intruder had walked Bradley Shaw's two remaining
thoroughbreds into clean stalls, supplied them with
fresh oats and water, then disappeared into the
night.

'Sure,' Brown said, 'but why would he do that?
Bodene Rich is dead, but we know from those two in
the cells they didn't fire the bunkhouse. If Danver's
still living out there, why bring the horses into town?'

'Sensible thing to do,' McReady said, not looking
up, 'would be to collect the first two horses and take
'em back out to BS Connected. Putting all four here
in town with George Plant costs money. So who's
paying? Not Danver, because he's seen both his
bosses die the hard way.'

He sat back and squinted at the notice he was
drafting on rough paper. It would be taken over to
the printers, where a flyer would be run off. It called
for anyone with fresh information relating to the
original attack on Red Booth to see the town
marshal.

McReady nodded his satisfaction, then tossed the
pencil onto the desk, picked up the paper and
handed it to Brown.

'Get a dozen copies run off pronto, tell the boy over there that when it's done he's to pin them up around town where people can read them. You ride out to BS Connected, find what the hell young Danver's up to.'

Brown got as far as the door, then stopped.

'More trouble,' he said. 'That was the Booths' buckboard that came in. It's across the street, loaded with what looks like all their worldly possessions – and you've got a visitor.'

And he stepped quickly out of the way as Frank Booth stormed into the jail.

'The same man who attacked my brother Red came calling,' Booth said, 'only this time he brought company.'

'And you were the target.'

McReady was sitting in his swivel chair, his visitor in a straight chair on the other side of the desk. Brown was standing by the door.

Booth was, McReady noticed, looking the worse for wear. As well as the black eye from his encounter with Bodene Rich, there was now an ugly swelling above his left ear. He had charged energetically enough into the office, but his movements had been stiff and he was clearly unsteady on his feet. When he'd dropped onto the chair there had been an audible grunt of relief.

'Three men, bags over their heads, slits for eyes,' he said. 'Would've been laughable if they hadn't been intent on violence. What makes it worse, the

85

attack was pointless. Me and Red, we were leaving anyway. We've had enough, were all packed and ready to go. Hell, the loaded buckboard was outside. They could see it, draw conclusions, and just to make sure we told them what we were doing. It made no difference.'

'Clubbing you with whatever it was they used was only pointless if it was Dieter Bauer's men ordering you off his land,' McReady said.

'It's possible it was Bauer's men. A couple of them, anyway. But if it was, last night they brought along a helper. A man with the right experience. A man who'd put his heart and soul behind club, boots and fists.'

McReady's eyes were narrowed thoughtfully. 'According to the verdict brought down six months ago in the courthouse over there,' he said, 'the man who attacked Red was Bodene Rich. If that's the kind of experience you're referring to, he's highly qualified.'

'None better. And Rich was there last night. It was Rich who attacked me, Rich who struck the first blow. I went out like a light, but I know from Red and the bruises on my body that he went ahead and gave me a good beating.'

'Bodene Rich?'

'Yes. Red watched him.'

'You said they had bags over their heads. How'd you two know it was Rich?'

Booth's laugh was bitter. ' "You're getting real good at this, Bodene, let's see what you can do with this one".'

McReady frowned. 'What?'

'I'm repeating what was said.'

'And that's why you think it was Rich?'

'Damn right. It couldn't have been clearer.'

'Why would he attack you? Where's the motive? You saying he was in Dieter Bauer's pay?'

'Could've been. But for Rich that'd be a bonus. He'd have come calling without Bauer's money, for the same motive as that first time. Red argued with him outside the Fat Lady. I attacked him over at the barn. He's a man who holds grudges.'

'No.' McReady shook his head. 'He was a man who held grudges.'

'What's that supposed to mean?'

'BS Connected was burnt to the ground. Bodene Rich had just bought the place, was enjoying his first night there. He was most likely asleep died in the fire. The two men who started it are back there in the cells reflecting on their sins.'

Frank Booth seemed to rock in the chair. His battered face registered disbelief.

'No, that can't be true,' he said. 'But if it is, why in God's name would three men attack me and blame it on a dead man?'

Spencer Hall was at the bar in the Fat Lady saloon when Dan McReady caught up with him. He was talking to Queenie Hart, but that buxom lady flounced away with a twirl of long red skirts, a sidelong smile and a flutter of long eyelashes when McReady stamped in. Turning his nose up at the

87

haze of cloying perfume that was drifting in her wake, McReady ordered a drink from the barman then accompanied Hall over to a corner table.

'I'm uneasy about my position in this town,' McReady said when they were sitting down. 'You were there by the barn when Rich rode into town. You heard him blame Al Ferris for the attack on Booth. Bad enough if I'd arrested the wrong man through a genuine mistake, but Rich later accused me of doing it for cash. Asked me who was slipping me greenbacks.'

'Bodene Rich is dead. Your worries are over.'

'You know that's not the way it works. Mud sticks. He was overheard both times, and people don't forget.'

'So why come to me?'

'Because as town marshal I'm always in the public eye. I'm the man with the badge, the man with the six-gun, the man who's responsible when law enforcement turns sour. I accept that. It goes with the job. What I don't accept is taking the can when another man is partly or wholly to blame.'

Hall, McReady noted, was wearing the face he took with him into the courtroom. His features gave nothing away, but no man is totally in control of his emotions. McReady, no mean judge of a man's reactions to the unexpected, saw the dapper lawyer's fingers tighten just a little around his shot glass.

'For a miscarriage of justice?' Hall smiled, then shook his head. 'Dan, all I did was present evidence in a court of law. The judge listened, his summing up damned Rich, the jury's verdict was unanimous.'

'No, you did more than that. The case against Rich was based on Liz Carter's evidence – she saw Rich near the Booth homestead – an argument Red Booth had with Rich and his saying, in court, that, yeah, he sort of figured it was Rich who attacked him. Pretty thin stuff.'

'As opposed to?'

'It's common knowledge Dieter Bauer wants the Booths off his land. That long-running feud's heavy stuff when compared to an argument between two liquored-up men outside the Fat Lady. And I've rarely heard more forceful arguments in any court than those you used to debunk the idea that Bauer was in any way connected to the attack on Booth.'

'So I'm Dieter Bauer's paid lackey?'

'You were in his corner, no doubt about it – and it's becoming pretty clear that Bodene Rich was innocent.'

'The man with new evidence to suggest that is dead, and any supporting evidence went with him to the grave.' Hall shrugged. 'Besides, who the hell cares? As I reminded you, Bodene Rich himself is dead.'

'Yeah,' McReady said, tossing back his drink and rising to leave. 'But if Rich was innocent, there's a guilty man out there – and, last night, Frank Booth was injured in an attack that was a carbon copy of the one on his brother.'

And, as he walked out, leaving Spencer Hall staring into space, Dan McReady was prepared to bet that it wouldn't be too long before a certain lawyer would be heading out for an urgent meeting with Dieter Bauer.

ELEVEN

On its course towards eventual union with the Gila River, Flats Creek meandered in a vague northerly direction. It was never too far away from the main road that led from Mesquite Flats to Yuma, but much closer to a less distinct trail which snaked across the Sheep Mountain foothills and turned towards the east. That route – known as the Logan Cut – was often used by swarthy armed men on horseback crossing the border from western Sonora and wanting, for a variety of shady reasons, to avoid the town, its lawmen and its penitentiary.

It was also, for other respectable travellers unconcerned about clashes with the law, a decent cross-country pathway which would eventually take them onto the main route to Phoenix, and just about wide enough to allow the passage of a reasonably sized wagon.

Bodene Rich had chosen as a campsite a stand of cottonwoods that was thriving on the relatively fertile land caught in one of Flats Creek's many ox-bow loops. If he put some effort into it, he reckoned, he could toss a good sized stone towards the Logan Cut and hit it first time – it was that close. The loop's opening faced the trail, the river enclosed what might be called the other three sides. When dawn broke, and a weary Matt Danver propped himself on an elbow to yawn and squint from his blankets, he quickly pointed out that the camp was a trap.

'That's one way of looking at it,' Rich said, intent on avoiding burnt fingers as he dangled a coffee pot from a forked stick over the crackling fire. 'Looked at from another angle, with an opening that narrow a dead man could hold off an army.'

Danver grinned, sat up and tugged on his boots.

'I was wondering about that. You reckon those two Easterners'll ride into the Flats with long faces, tell the town of its sad loss?'

'Bound to. I've got the feeling they've already told McReady I owe them a heap of money. They'll probably go see Spencer Hall and claim that, with me dead, they now own the BS Connected.'

'And I get another new boss. Dammit, I'm beginning to feel dizzy.'

Danver finished strapping his bedroll, stepped close to the fire, poured coffee from the bubbling pot into two cups and handed one to Rich.

'We moved off BS Connected, so I can see the sense in taking the horses into town,' he said. 'But the bunkhouse is still standing, and if you reckon they're going to claim the spread I don't understand why the hell we didn't stay put. Or why you didn't

92

leave me to mind the store, ride into town and get McReady to arrest those fellers for attempted murder.'

'The answer to both is, right now it's convenient for me to stay dead.'

'Because. . . ?'

Now Rich grinned.

'Because I'm not – but if everybody believes I am it'll be easier to find out who attacked Red Booth.'

'Why bother? You were set free. Why not leave it at that?'

'You know damn well why. I can shout my innocence from the top of Sheep Mountain but, unless I can prove another man's guilt, there'll be a shadow hanging over me for the rest of my life. I like it here in western Arizona. I've bought a decent spread, and you're going to help me breed the finest palominos in the territory, but as things stand now my name has been blackened. As long as it stays that way, there's no chance I'll ever be accepted in Mesquite Flats.'

Pete McReady picked up the stink of the fire when he was a good half mile from BS Connected. His horse at once became twitchy, and he was forced to coax the nervous animal across the blue-grass slope in front of what had been the ranch house and leave it hitched to a shrub some way from the blackened ruins.

Curls of white smoke still rose from the ashes. Blackened beams lay like the rotting bones of long dead mammoths. Huge stones used to construct the chimney had split in the intense heat, and as Pete drew nearer he knew that it would be some time yet before a close inspection became possible.

Thumb hitched in his gunbelt, he circled what was left of the house, walking anti-clockwise and squinting his right eye against the still fierce heat. As best he could from a distance he was running his gaze over the ashes looking for the white of human bones, the glint of metal that could be Bodene Rich's six-gun, belt buckle, spurs. . . .

He had given up long before he had completed his circuit, and it was then that he saw – in the soft dirt behind the house – the signs that two horses had passed that way.

'Well now,' the deputy said softly, and he lifted his gaze from the hoof prints to the slope leading to a stand of pines and, above that, the high rimrock.

It took him almost half an hour to follow, on foot, the route the horses had taken. When he emerged from the cleft in the rock onto the high ground and felt the weight of the sun's direct heat, he was breathing hard. He took off his Stetson and fanned his face, all the while walking slowly, studying the ground. He found where the horses had been standing, judged from the state of the ground that they had been there for some time. And close to the rimrock it became clear from the scuffing in the dry dust and the crushed cigarette ends that the two men – Bodene Rich and Matt Danver – had waited patiently.

Waited patiently for the arrival of the two men from back East, Pete thought, walking to the edge of the rimrock and gazing into the distance. Danver had been in town. He'd seen the Thackrays talking to Dan, and reported to Rich. Rich knew they would come after him.

'But I'll bet he didn't know they'd burn down his new home,' Pete said softly. 'Any more than he could have known that the very next day I'd be up here looking at where he and that young wrangler have set up camp.'

And with a final glance through the shimmering heat haze at the thin pencil of smoke rising from the distant ox-bow on Flats Creek, Pete McReady started back down the steep slope.

He had noticed one item of interest as he walked around the smoking ruins, and that was a gallon can that had been carelessly tossed to one side. The screw top was missing. A sniff told Pete that the can had contained kerosene. He walked across the blue grass to his horse, used a rawhide thong to tie the can behind the cantle, then flipped the reins back over the horse's head and swung into the saddle.

As he did so, he heard the rattle of gunfire.

Distant. Shrewdly, yet not knowing why, he placed the sound as coming from the distant ox-bow. With his brow furrowed in thought, he hesitated for a few moments. Then, shaking his head, he touched his horse's flanks with his heels and set off for Mesquite Flats at a brisk canter.

Pete McReady took almost an hour to reach Dieter

Bauer's run-down spread. He rode at a pace that was dictated not by his enjoyment of a fine morning, but by reluctance: he was not looking forward to his encounter with the short-tempered and often violent rancher. Getting Bauer to talk civilly was always difficult. Getting around him to talk to his wife, in private, was going to need some smooth talking.

The ride into the spread was down a rutted trail. The yard that was a flat open space between house, barns and bunkhouse was deserted. Behind the barns and the big corral the land sloped gradually for a mile or so to Flats Creek and the Booths' homestead. Beyond that, Sheep Mountain was a jagged outline against almost white skies. Squinting into that searing light, Pete thought he could just make out, in the foothills, the blackened shape that was the remains of Bradley Shaw's ranch house – but he knew that was probably his imagination.

As he rode in, Bauer emerged from the shadows deep inside one of the open barns. He was accompanied by Al Ferris. The big foreman was wiping his hands on a rag. He stared at Pete, spat, then flung the rag behind him and strolled towards the corral.

'Dieter,' Pete said, nodding to the rancher.

He swung down, loosely tied his horse to the rail in front of the house.

'What now?' Bauer said, hands on hips.

'Couple of things.' Pete stripped off his gloves. 'I guess you know Bodene Rich is dead?'

The look on Bauer's face caused Pete to smile inwardly. The rancher *hadn't* known, and was shocked, but the shock was immediately followed by a narrowing of the cold, calculating eyes as Bauer thought fast. There could be only one reason for that. If Bauer had been behind the attack on Frank Booth, he had deliberately set out to pin the blame on Rich. Now he needed to know if Bodene Rich had died before or after that attack.

'Before,' Pete said – and waited.

After a moment, Bauer said, 'What the hell are you talking about?'

'Rich died before Frank Booth was set upon by three men, and hurt bad.'

'What am I supposed to do, applaud? So Rich didn't attack Frank Booth. So what? That doesn't change what happened in the past.'

'What happened six months ago has already been altered by Rich's early release. But the men who did attack Frank are still living in the past, and didn't know Rich had died in the fire. One of them addressed a companion as Bodene.'

'Then find that person.'

'We intend to.' Pete said. 'That's why I'm here. Your wife was probably Bradley Shaw's only local confidant—'

'What the hell's that?'

'They met from time to time, and it's no secret he confided in her. He may have let slip the reasons behind Rich's release, so with your permission I'd like to talk to Ellie.'

'You're wasting your time.'

'Until I talk to her you can't possibly know—'

'She's not here. You rode out here with nothing, you'll ride back with the same.'

'If she's in town, we'll talk to her there.'

'She hasn't been home. I don't know where she is.'

'You mean she's missing?' Pete said, and felt a cold tingle along his spine as he remembered the two men coming out of the barn, Ferris wiping his hands on a rag.

'What I mean is she could be a thousand miles away by now. She handled the spread's accounts. I've done some quick checks. Over the past year or so there's sums of money been taken out, regularly, for no damn reason that I could see. That explains why my finances are shot to hell, tells you why I believe she's gone for good.'

'She's not the only one,' Pete said, turning towards his horse, swinging into the saddle but keeping a keen eye on Bauer. 'Red and Frank Booth have loaded up and moved out. The second attack was the last straw, so, involved or not you got your wish and they're finally off your land.'

TWELVE

Dieter Bauer rode into town some way behind Pete McReady. He watched Dan's son tie his horse and cross the plank walk into the jail, then pushed on up the street to Spencer Hall's office. The room was empty. Bauer followed the trail of cigar smoke through the back room. Hall was in the yard, ripping up a stack of documents and cramming them into a sack.

'Anticipating an inspection, or just feeling guilty?'

'They pile up. If I didn't move them from time to time I'd be squeezed out onto the street.'

'Sound must travel a fair distance hereabouts,' Bauer said, 'because I was saying something similar to myself on my way into town. Likely to be squeezed out of my place, that is. But not from lack of space, because of a shortage of cash. Ellie's been bleeding us dry.'

Hall stared. 'Ellie has?'

Bauer's face was placid. 'Leastwise, that's what I told Pete McReady. She's gone missing, so I thought

I'd better start dishing out the explanations before someone over at John Thorpe's bank looks too deeply into my affairs.'

'Dishing out the lies, you mean.' Hall tied the top of the sack with cord and brushed past Bauer. 'You've been handing that cash to me for services rendered.'

'Yeah, but Ellie's been drawing it from the bank.'

'To pay the men. And if that didn't get done, you blamed Ellie when she wasn't around to hear.'

They'd moved into the office. Hall had swept up his smouldering cigar from an ashtray in the back room. He dropped heavily into the leather swivel chair behind the desk. Bauer stayed on his feet.

'The money you give me keeps Al Ferris out of jail, it doesn't buy my body, my soul,' Hall said. 'You can spread your lies like quicklime all over town, but they'll do nothing to kill suspicion – and Dan McReady's made it clear he's suspects me of taking cash to make sure Rich was convicted. So it ends now.'

'I agree. Seems it's over. Bodene Rich is dead, the Booths have moved off my land, far as I'm concerned everything's been put to bed.'

'Except for two things. I don't think the new evidence that came to light died with Bradley Shaw, and I've got to come up with some way of dealing with Dan McReady's suspicions.'

'So saying it ends now was a mite premature,' Bauer said. 'You're looking at a stick of dynamite with the fuse spluttering, I've got a foreman who, a few years back, saved my life. He naturally expects me to do the same for him, which is what I've being doing thus far.'

He sat down, then reached across the desk to take a cigar from the cuspidor and poke it into the top pocket of his shirt.

Hall's lips were pursed, his eyes thoughtful. 'Sounds to me,' he said, 'as if those two outstanding problems are inextricably linked.'

'Big words always did have me foxed,' Bauer said, 'but if it's something to do with mutual back scratching then I tend to agree.'

'Dan McReady's a widower, lives with son Pete in a house on the edge of town,' Hall said, studying the tip of his cigar. 'Pete spends evenings here in town, on duty at the jail, or up against the bar in the Fat Lady. Means his father's often alone in the house.' He looked up, met Bauer's sardonic gaze. 'If, by some means, you could arrange it so that it became impossible for McReady to pass on his suspicions, I see no reason why our business relationship cannot remain on the same footing.'

'I can,' Bauer said bluntly. 'If I arrange it so McReady meets a sticky end – so he's permanently out of your hair – that counts as payment for all future services. You get no more cash.'

'Arrange it?'

'Someone else pulls the trigger. I'm in the clear.'

'As always.' Hall smiled. 'You realize I could still be the winner. All suspicion removed, and if this new evidence comes to nought you may never again need the help of a lawyer.'

'But if I do. . . ?'

'Mutual back scratching, mutual trust,' Hall said, and he leaned across the desk and extended his hand. 'Deal?'

'Deal,' Dieter Bauer said. 'This time tomorrow, Mesquite Flat's town council will be advertising for a new marshal.'

'First thing is, I don't believe Bodene Rich died in the fire.'

'No sign of a body?' McReady said.

Brown ripped off his bandanna, wiped dust and sweat from his glistening face, and sat down.

'Nope. Seems he was expecting those boys from back East. Him and Danver rode up to the rimrock.'

'How sure are you?'

'The horse Rich is riding's got a rear shoe with a chunk of iron missing. The tracks were clear. Could've been someone else riding his horse – but, no, it was him all right.'

'So he rode up the hill with the wrangler, watched the Thackrays without a chance of being seen.' McReady nodded. 'Unfortunately, that ride to the high ground put him too far away to do anything to stop them burning down his house.'

'Matt Danver's good with a rifle.'

'Yeah, but they were puzzled, wondered what was going to happen when the Thackrays snuck up to the house. By the time they smelled smoke, saw flames, it was too late.'

Brown nodded. 'Second thing is, I think I know

102

where Rich is now.'

'Then you've better keep your voice down. I'd hate for those boys out back to overhear.'

'Not much they can do when they're gazing at the world through strap-steel bars.'

'True, but things are changing fast. If Rich is alive, all I've got those Easterners for is arson, and the town council'd rather not be buying two grown men three meals a day.'

'You could still hold them for attempted murder.'

'No. Hall would get them off. They'd claim they saw Rich and Danver ride up the hill, knew the house was empty.' He spun his chair, hoisted his boots onto the desk. 'So, where is Rich?'

'First Flats Creek loop. The ox-bow a couple of miles downstream from the Bauer spread.'

'I know it. So . . . what? You go down there looking for him?'

'I climbed to the rimrock to make damn sure I'd read the signs right. From there I spotted the smoke from a camp-fire.'

McReady frowned. 'Could be a drifter. Or a couple of swarthy characters from the south, wearing fancy sombreros and whiskers and eyeing what's left of Bauer's herd.'

'Whoever's out there,' Brown said languidly, 'ran into trouble. I rode away from BS Connected with the sound of gunfire ringing in my ears.'

'Dammit,' McReady said fiercely. He swung his boots down, spun the chair one way, then the other, got to his feet and whirled it with his hand. 'The

Booths have moved out. They took their wagon down the Logan Cut, and the Cut—'

'Passes mighty close to that ox-bow.'

'Too late to put a stop to it now—'

'Why bother? A few dead bodies out there would solve at least some of your problems.'

McReady paced, frowning, ran his fingers through his hair, then turned quickly. His son's lean figure had sent a shadow flitting across the office as he came in out of the bright sunlight.

'I suppose you've brought more trouble?'

'Ellie's missing,' Pete said.

'Thank Christ,' McReady said. 'That's not a problem, it's a blessing.'

'Damn right,' Brown said. 'It's a wonder she didn't take herself off years ago.'

Pete nodded cautiously. 'According to Bauer, there's some planning gone into this. She's been siphoning money out of the spread's accounts, built herself a nice nest egg and lit out. However. . . .'

Dan rolled his eyes. 'Go on.'

'That could be a story cooked up by Bauer to hide the fact that he's done away with her.'

'You got a reason for even suggesting that?'

'Something about the two of them, Bauer and Al Ferris. In particular, the way Ferris was acting when he came out of the barn.' He shrugged. 'Forget I said anything. I always get the shivers when I'm too close to Dieter Bauer.'

'What we'll do is wait, see if she shows up in a couple of days,' McReady said. 'Right now I've got two prisoners I want out of here, so I'll rattle some keys, tell the Thackrays they're free to go.' He grimaced. 'I'll tell 'em why, and hope to hell I'm right. Pete, Vern will tell you all about his trip out to BS Connected. When he's done that I want you two to get something to eat, then ride along Logan's Cut to the ox-bow, see if Rich has survived what could've been a second attempt to put him six feet under.'

THIRTEEN

'Yeah, it's smoke, and it's from a camp-fire. Somebody's out there on the ox-bow.'

Red Booth was squinting into the bright sunlight. They'd been trundling steadily along Logan's cut. The heat was like a heavy woollen blanket sucking the sweat from their pores, the waters of Flats Creek a cool inviting ribbon of silver down the slope to their right. Then Frank had seen the thin pencil of white smoke rising above the grey-green leaves of the cottonwoods where the river looped. He'd tightened his grip on the reins. The buckboard slowed. There was a soft whicker of protest from the two horses tied behind the wagon. Then the buckboard ground to a halt.

'Whoever it is,' Frank Booth said after a moment, 'they're no concern of ours, unlikely to cause trouble.'

'Then why did you stop?'

'Cautious. We've both taken a battering. But, thinking about it, I know a lot of ordinary folk use this trail. Could be a family heading north, stopped there for the night and the mother's cooking them a late breakfast.'

'Could be Apaches,' Red said, 'and then they'll deal us a whole heap of trouble.'

Frank laughed. 'Geronimo's boys have given up the fight. Besides, Apaches are not going to light a fire that sends smoke up so every white man within a ten mile circle knows where they are.'

'I can see someone moving about. Too hot, too far away make 'em out. You got those glasses handy?'

Frank leaned back over the seat, stretched behind him and came up with an ancient pair of field-glasses. He put them to his eyes, fiddled with the knurled focusing knob.

'Well I'll be double damned,' he said softly. 'I'm looking at a dead man.'

'What—?

'That feller you can see moving is Bodene Rich.'

'No, you must be wrong.' Red stared at his brother as he lowered the glasses. 'Hell, Frank, we passed BS Connected a half hour ago. Shaw's house is a smouldering ruin.'

'Yeah, but we've only got McReady's word Rich was in there when it went up in flames.'

Red snatched at the glasses. His lips were a thin line as he lifted them to his eyes. Then, after a leaden minute of utter silence, suddenly he was smiling. The smile was ugly. He tossed the glasses back to his brother, twisted and bent down. From under the seat he dragged the leather saddle boot holding his

Winchester rifle. He drew out the glittering weapon then scrambled over the seat. There was just room behind it for him to go down on his knees. There was a metallic snap as he worked a shell into the breech. Using the seat back as a support for his elbows, he settled the rifle's butt snug against his shoulder, put his cheek to the polished stock and squinted along the sights.

Frank's face was grim. He opened his mouth as if to protest, then clamped it shut and again raised the glasses.

The horse standing in the wagon's traces jerked as the shot cracked, shattering the stillness. The heat-haze was so dense that it was almost as if both men could see the hot air parting and follow the bullet's flight to its target. But that was an illusion.

Red Booth lifted his head, looked questioningly at his brother.

'I saw him go down,' he said, 'but I'm not sure if I hit him.'

'Any man would go down,' Frank said tightly, 'when a .44-.40 slug whistles within an inch of—'

Before he could finish speaking there was a bright muzzle-flash at the narrow opening to the ox-bow, followed by another and yet another. Then the brittle crack of the three shots reached them, and both men ducked instinctively as bullets hissed through the air above their heads.

'So I missed,' Red Booth said grimly, 'and now we've got a fight on our hands.'

'No, wait.'

Red half-lowered the rifle, frowned. Frank realized he was looking at him strangely. Not directly at him – but at his head; at the old scar above his ear. Suddenly he took a deep breath, held it, folded both hands across his mouth and closed his eyes.

'Something wrong?'

Frank nodded slowly, without opening his eyes. He reached up and gingerly touched the fresh, painful swelling on his own head, then shook his head and looked at his brother. His face wore a haunted expression.

'Something's been bothering me for a while now,' he said, 'and I couldn't figure out what it was. But now, looking at you, looking at the scar where you were bludgeoned, remembering what happened to me and how it was . . . Red, suddenly it came to me, and if I'm right about this we made a terrible mistake six months ago, and damned if we didn't do the same again when we were talking to Dan McReady.'

'They're coming in,' Bodene Rich said. 'One of them's waving a white flag.'

'A slug parts your hair, I send three warning shots over their heads – and they give up?'

There was a rough, overgrown track of sorts leading onto the land enclosed by the ox-bow which suggested that it had been used as a resting place from the dawn of time. An oasis, Rich thought with some amusement, and he watched the incoming Booths bring the buckboard in just so far, decide they'd have difficulty turning it, and pull to a halt just off the Logan Cut. A wheel dropped into a rut that could have been centuries old. The wagon tilted, settled.

Red tossed the stick with its makeshift flag of truce behind him, both men jumped down – Red less nimbly – and walked towards Rich and Danver. Left the white flag, Rich noted, but brought along the Winchester. Frank's unarmed. Looks troubled.

'Things could've turned nasty,' Red Booth said as they approached, 'if my brother hadn't got brain fever and called a halt. He's figured something out, says we've made real bad mistakes—'

'Been forced into making wrong assumptions by a lawyer with a silver tongue,' Frank Booth said. He looked at Rich. 'Why don't we see what's left in your coffee pot, then I'll tell you what's on my mind?'

Danver was also keeping his Winchester at the ready. The tang of cordite hung in the hot air, a reminder that they had all been on the brink of violent confrontation. Hanging on to the rifle with his left hand, the wrangler spilled steaming coffee into the cups he and Rich had been using and handed them one by one to the Booths. All four men moved away from the heat of the fire. In the shade of the cottonwoods they sat on logs, or cross-legged in the rough, dry grass. Danver sat some yards outside the circle. His back was to a tree, the rifle across his thighs. Insects hummed. Flats Creek encircled them. It was a soothing ripple of sound that did nothing to ease the tension.

'So what's all this about mistakes made?' Rich said.

110

'You had six months in a Yuma cell. I'm surprised that in all that time you didn't work it out for yourself.'

'Work what out, Frank? That your brother was wrong pointing the finger at me? Hell, I didn't need six *minutes*, never mind six months. I was nowhere *near* your brother the night he was attacked.'

'Yeah, but shouting that in court got you nowhere. What you needed was something that could be understood by the man serving beer in the Fat Lady, by the kid' – he turned to grin at Matt Danver – 'working horses for an old prison warden.'

'Or by a man worked over so bad he'll spend the rest of his life limping,' Red Booth said. 'For Christ's sake, Frank, get on with it.'

'Danver,' Frank Booth said, 'get up on your feet and hold that rifle by the barrel so you can swing it like a club. Red, go stand with your back to him.'

Both men got to their feet, Danver smoothly, Red Booth with some difficulty. They came together. Red Booth turned his back to Danver. The wrangler looked across at Frank.

'OK, now show us how you'd use that club. You're attacking a man from behind, you want to club him to the ground. Demonstrate how you'd go about it – placing the butt of the rifle exactly where you'd strike the blow.'

Danver grimaced. He looked at Rich, who shrugged. Then the wrangler lifted the rifle, held it like a club with his hands clasping the barrel, and moved it in a slow, sweeping swing to rest against the side of Red Booth's head.

'And there,' Frank Booth said softly, 'you have it.'

For a moment there was silence. Then Bodene Rich exploded.

'Jesus Christ,' he said, springing to his feet. 'Red was felled by a blow delivered from behind – but the blow struck the left side of his head.'

'Exactly. The man who attacked him had to be—'

'Left-handed,' Matt Danver said, lowering the rifle and stepping back.

'The man who attacked *both* of us was left-handed,' Frank Booth said, 'and from the confrontation we had outside Plant's barn I know for sure that you, Rich, favour your right.'

'So who fits?' Red Booth said thickly. 'If I've been looking at the wrong man this whole time – who should I have had in my sights?'

'That's an easy one,' Matt Danver said. 'I went to school with the only leftie I know in these parts: his name's Kris Bauer.'

FOURTEEN

Pete McReady and Vern Brown reached the ox-bow late in the day. Both men had eaten well, then decided that to see them through the long ride in the afternoon sun their bodies required liquid reserves. That had been given to them in glasses passed across the bar in the Fat Lady saloon by Queenie Hart, who had long ago taken a shine to the older Vern Brown.

The deputies had been in no hurry. Between drinks, Pete mused on the number of shots he'd heard when at the BS Connected, reckoned he'd counted no more than half a dozen. He was unconcerned. Out at the ox-bow, what happened had happened. They would investigate, but nothing would change.

In the event, there was nothing for the lawmen to investigate – though that was not immediately obvious. They saw the Booths' buckboard from afar as they rode in. It was tilted drunkenly, there was no sign of life; not a good omen. They passed it cautiously, rode across the coarse grass towards the cottonwoods caught in the creek's loop and saw the white remains of a fire, a coffee pot hanging over dead embers and, at the edge of the trees, four men lying motionless in the shade.

Bodies, Pete McReady thought, and in that instant he felt his hair prickle as he pictured a gunfight that left all four participants dead. When he caught the shine of half-open eyes he was not reassured, having more than once been fooled into imagining the presence of life when a corpse had gazed at him through eyelids like clogged knife slits.

Then Bodene Rich sat up – just about stopping Pete's heart – yawned, and with blithe indifference told the two deputies that he'd been tracking their approach all the way from BS Connected, had early on seen the glint of their badges, and settled into a pleasant doze while awaiting their arrival.

McReady and Brown sat on the warm shale at the edge of the creek as Bodene Rich told them how Frank Booth's startling theory knocked all previous evidence and rulings into a cocked hat. At first sceptical, they quickly came around to Rich's way of thinking when he staged his own demonstration, using Vern Brown as victim. When the tableau broke up, Brown and McReady exchanged looks. Rich knew that as small-town lawmen they had at once made the leap to Spencer Hall, and the realization that no lawyer worth his salt could have missed such

114

a glaring error.

'Depends on who was at the crime scene, and if that man had eyes to see what was staring him in the face,' Rich said quietly, knowing it had been Marshal Dan McReady, and knowing too that neither deputy would say so. 'Or, looked at another way,' Rich said, 'depends on who was paying the lawyer to convict a scapegoat. And as young Kris Bauer is now looking as guilty as hell, it's not hard to work out who was filling Hall's pockets with hard cash.'

'Dieter Bauer,' Pete McReady said tightly. 'And we'll get around to him and his son, but right now there's no call for us to rush because there's no reason for them to get jumpy. Bradley Shaw was gunned down, as far as they know you died in the fire, and the Booths have moved off their land. They'll be convinced they're sitting pretty, so first we head back to town, talk to my pa.'

'I don't think we should waste too much time,' Vern Brown said. 'Ellie's gone missing, and I didn't see Kris when I was out at the Bauer place. Bradley Shaw had hold of new evidence. If he confided in Ellie she could have warned her son the game was up.'

'You're right, let's get the hell out of here,' Pete McReady said. He turned, crunched away across the shale, called over his shoulder, 'We move fast, but nothing's changed: town first, talk to Pa, then only if he swallows Rich's story do we go after the Bauers.'

His words trailed in his wake. Brown nodded

115

curtly to Rich, but didn't at once follow his fellow deputy. He looked at Rich, hesitating, seemed about to say something but kept his mouth tightly clamped.

'Let me say it for you,' Rich said. 'You want Kris Bauer in jail, but you think the story about the attacker being a man who favours his left hand will carry more weight if I'm there to tell it.'

'I think it'd be a good idea. Since you got let out of jail on evidence nobody's seen, Dan's been wary of taking anything on trust – and, despite what Pete told him, he still doesn't know for sure if you're alive or dead.'

'I've got obvious personal reasons for wanting Kris Bauer arrested, and for being there to watch it happen. Go ahead, catch up with your partner. I'll let the Booths know what's going on; right now they're undecided about keeping going, or returning to their home on Flats Creek. Matt Danver will ride with me into town.'

Rich's smile was grim. 'I hate to say it, but an uneasy feeling in my gut tells me nothing about this is going to be straightforward.'

The coffee-pot was bubbling on the iron stove with that peculiar hissing and crackling that warns that it's close to boiling dry. The strong smell of the over-heated grounds filled the office. The oil lamp hanging almost directly over the desk had begun swinging in the draught when Pete McReady opened the office door, casting dark shifting shadows across the chairs, the gleaming weapons in the gun cabinet, the file cabinets, the desk, and the man who was slumped bloodily in the swivel chair.

Dan McReady was staring out of sightless eyes, the blood from the terrible wound on the side of his head soaking his shirt from his shoulder all the way down his right arm to the buttoned cuff. His hand hung loose. Congealing blood was dripping thickly from limp fingers, pooling red on the floor.

'Not been dead long,' Pete McReady said in a choked voice. 'The son of a bitch, the *stinking son of a bitch*, he used a club because a bullet would have been heard. This way he could walk in, murder my pa, then walk out with a false smile on his face as if he'd been chewing the fat with a close friend.'

'Maybe it *was* someone Dan considered a friend,' Vern Brown said, and he stepped forward to put a comforting hand on Pete's shoulder. 'Certainly it was someone he knew, had to be for him to sit there and take it without moving a muscle in his defence.'

'Someone we all know,' Bodene Rich said, circling around so that he could see clearly. 'Look at the wound. Right side of the head. We've been through this out at the ox-bow. Attacking from behind, a left-handed man hits the left side of the head, from the front it's the right side and that's what we've got here. The man who did this attacked Red Booth six months ago, Frank Booth within the last twenty-four hours, Dan McReady less than an hour ago.'

'Kris Bauer?'

'We can't be sure, can't risk jumping to conclusions when what's at stake is a young man's life – but, yeah, that's the way it's looking.'

'But why Dan? What the hell has my pa ever done to harm that kid?'

Pete had twisted away from the desk, from his dead father. His face was grey.

'We'll know when we ask him,' Brown said. 'We'll ride out there and ask him, he'll tell us, then we'll hang him from the nearest tree.'

He was still holding Pete's shoulder. He gently shook the young deputy, looked into his wet eyes.

'Get yourself up the street to the Fat Lady,' he said softly. 'You need a stiff drink—'

'You go with him,' Bodene Rich said. He glanced across at Danver, who was standing silent and sombre in the doorway. 'Matt will find Ben Laing, he'll look after Dan, take him away, clean him up and lay him out decent. I'll go and talk to Spencer Hall – doesn't he live over his office?'

'Why Hall?' Brown, walking with Pete to the door, was frowning.

'Hall advises the council, so he needs to know what's happened. You need a new marshal, and the transfer of power has to be legal and above board.'

He watched Brown and Pete McReady on their way to Queenie's saloon, nodded to Matt Danver who headed down the street in the opposite direction to alert the undertaker. Then, with a final glance at Dan McReady, caught and held in the slowly moving circle of light from the hanging oil lamp, Rich set off across the street.

Immediately, while still taking those first few bold strides, he experienced that same disconcerting feeling of being watched, of being observed by someone squinting at him along the sights of a powerful rifle. On the previous occasion he had been driving out of town on Bradley Shaw's top-buggy and the person he feared was Red Booth's brother. This time it was the Thackrays. Dan McReady had let them out of jail, and Rich knew damn well that by now they'd have learned that their attempt to burn him to death had failed. So they'd try again, and yet again if necessary; and what better way could there be of killing a man than waiting at an upper storey window, with a rifle, until the lone figure walked out of the shadows and into the lamplight?

Then, with a somewhat sheepish grin, Bodene Rich gave himself a mental shake, squared his shoulders, and set his mind resolutely to the tasks that lay ahead.

There was a light in the window above Spencer Hall's office door. Rich shouted the lawyer's name, waited, got no response so stepped forward and used his fist to hammer on the door. That elicited an angry shout. Footsteps thumped down the stairs. The door was flung open.

'We need to talk,' Bodene Rich said, and pushed his way into the shadowy office.

Hall let a breath out explosively. In black pants and under-vest, hair unkempt, he padded after Rich on bare feet.

'Dan McReady's dead,' Rich said, swinging round

119

with his back to the desk.

Hall froze. The only light was that filtering in from the street-lamps and the open door of the Fat Lady saloon across the way, but Rich thought the lawyer had turned pale.

'How can that be?' Hall said. 'I've been here in the office, or upstairs, since late afternoon. I saw Dan cross the street just before dark. If there'd been shots, I'd have heard them—'

'He was clubbed to death.'

'Ah. And . . . you've got an alibi?'

'Damn you, Hall,' Rich said tightly.

'You're the one could be damned,' Hall said, 'because we both know the conclusion the citizens of this town will jump to when they find out McReady's been killed, in that brutal manner, a couple of days after you show up.'

'By the time the news gets out, McReady's killer will be behind bars. I'm riding out with Vern Brown and Matt Danver. As senior deputy, I guess you'll agree to Brown standing in as town marshal. His first job will be to arrest Kris Bauer.'

Hall's widened eyes showed white in the dim light. Abruptly he padded around Rich, opened a desk drawer and took out a whiskey bottle. He popped the cork, gulped down a quick drink.

'What the hell are you talking about?' he said hoarsely.

'It's been demonstrated to Brown and Pete McReady that the man who attacked the Booths, and murdered Dan McReady, is left handed – and Danver went to school with Kris Bauer.'

'Kris Bauer's left handed, sure, but. . . .'

Even in that unlighted room Rich could see a whole range of emotions flicker across Hall's pale face. For a long moment the lawyer stood stock still. Then he placed the whiskey bottle on the desk, dropped into the swivel chair and gazed abstractedly towards the window.

'Sure had me fooled,' he said, almost inaudibly, as if thinking out loud. 'For months I've been wondering why he. . . .'

Again he broke off, his lips tight.

'You're beginning to annoy me, Hall. What have you been wondering – and about who?'

'Nothing, it's not important.' He stared at Rich. 'Al Ferris was a name that came up when you were in court. I guess this left-handed theory gets him off the hook.'

'You're the lawyer,' Rich said, 'and as you got me convicted you must be pretty good at your job – but if I were you I wouldn't volunteer to defend Kris Bauer.'

'Kris Bauer,' Spencer Hall said softly, 'will never appear in court.'

Rich hesitated, again wondering what the hell the lawyer was talking about. Then he flapped a dismissive hand and turned away. Through the still open door he saw that Vern Brown was leaving the bright lights of the Fat Lady. Feeling the first exhilarating rush of adrenaline through his veins as a piano jangled discordantly and raucous laughter split the night air, Rich deliberately slammed Hall's door on his way out and jogged across the street to join the deputy.

FIFTEEN

They rode hard to the Bauer spread, Rich, Vern Brown and Matt Danver. Pete McReady stayed in town. There was his pa's funeral to arrange. Besides, the experienced Vern Brown was of the opinion that, in his present angry and distressed state of mind, the young deputy was liable to pull his pistol and fire at the first thing that moved.

They rode in darkness unbroken by moonlight, for cloud cover blanketed the land and intensified the grave and gloomy mood that hung over the four men. There had been a short discussion about adding to their numbers if they had to hunt for Kris Bauer. Vern Brown, as acting marshal, the makeshift posse's leader, stated bluntly that if four grown men couldn't overpower a kid of nineteen years they should take up sheepherding.

Danver, himself just twenty, had grinned into the darkness.

Their approach was far from stealthy. Bauer was out in the yard when they hammered in raising clouds of dust, waiting with hands on hips. The four men drew rein. Brown eased his mount close to the rancher, sat with hands folded on the horn.

'We've come for your son, Dieter. We've reason to believe he was involved in the attacks on Red and Frank Booth, and in the murder of Dan McReady.'

'What about Bradley Shaw, ain't you tryin' to pin that one on him?' He spat. 'Anyway, you're way too late. Ferris saw him ride out, late afternoon. But if you think you can pin McReady's killing on him, you're wrong. Kris was long gone. Ferris reckons he was heading for the Logan Cut, after that, who knows?'

'Where's Ferris now?'

'In bed, dreaming about the painted girls in the Yuma dance halls.'

'So I'll take his word for it, but the direction Kris took means nothing, he could have circled round to deal with McReady,' Brown said bluntly. 'Anyhow, talk's wasting time—'

'I'll ride with you.'

'That's not necessary.'

'Some posses figure a bullet in the head is a good way to avoid wasting time in a court of law. You find him, I want to be there to stand between you and my boy.'

He was walking and talking, hurrying across the yard to the barn. Rich could see no sign of life anywhere, no sign of Ellie Bauer, no sign of Al Ferris so maybe the man *was* asleep.

'I notice Bauer wasn't shocked by news of Dan's

death,' Brown said pointedly.

'A little bird must've sung in his ear,' Rich said. 'But which little bird?'

'Yeah, and you realize if he rides with us we've got an enemy inside and outside the tent?'

'If Kris is using the Logan Cut, it's possible he'll be seen by the Booths. They recognize him in time, they'll hold him there at the ox-bow.'

Brown laughed. 'Don't hold your breath.'

Harness jingled in the darkness. They heard the snort of a horse. Then Bauer reappeared. He was on a rangy gelding with bulky saddle-bags, and was tucking a shotgun into its leather boot under his thigh. Never did wear a gunbelt, Rich realized, and for an instant he wondered why.

Then Bauer straightened up, flashed them a fierce grin, and the night pulsed to the drum of hoofs as the five men thundered out of the yard.

Maybe the Booths figured that the bigger the fire, the more chance there was of convincing marauding Apaches that it was a sizeable military encampment. They must have chopped down a good section of forest for fuel. Sparks were flying high above the cottonwoods, and dancing flames lit up the encircling trees as Bodene Rich led the way past the canted buckboard and onto the ox-bow.

Frank and Red were sitting ten feet back from the blazing fire. They had cups in their hands, but there was no sign of a coffee pot. Knocking back stronger stuff, Rich surmised, and was mildly amused when

Frank lurched sideways unsteadily when he stood up.

'No sign of him, so I guess he rode on through?' Rich said, raising his voice above the fierce crackling. 'If he came this way.'

'Sure he did. *They* did. Kris Bauer and the foreman, Ferris. We were down at the creek, washing pots. Just about dark by then, but the fire was already going strong. They were outside the circle of light. Red recognized them, but too late to act.'

'Not up to us anyway,' Red said, twisting to look at them. 'I've had a bellyful of Bauers, and Ferris is one mean son of a bitch.'

'So, what's that?' Brown said. 'Dark when they rode through, three hours or more they've got on us?'

'Yeah, but Kris's horse was lame,' Frank said.

'That helps,' Brown said, 'but I'm getting bad feelings about this.'

Rich flashed him a look. 'If Kris was here when it was just about dark, there's no way he could have killed McReady – is that what you mean?'

'What do you think?'

'I think you're right.'

'I told you before we rode out,' Dieter Bauer said, 'but you wouldn't listen.'

'You also told us Ferris was asleep,' Rich said. 'That was a lie. What you didn't tell us is how you knew Dan McReady was dead.'

'Ferris was in town, brought the news.'

'Another lie. Al Ferris is with your son.'

'No, that's the truth. It was me saw Kris ride out,

not Ferris. Later, when Ferris got back from town, I sent him after Kris.'

'And he caught him? You think that's possible?'

'If Kris's horse went lame – yes.'

Brown stirred restlessly in the saddle.

'There's only one way of settling this.'

'Yes, and once again we're wasting time.' Rich nodded. 'What about Bauer? I say he stays here. Al Ferris being with Kris changes the odds.'

'And Ferris being in town at the right time means he's back as a suspect,' Brown said. 'If he's guilty, he's going to be a desperate man.'

'Then you need me,' Dieter Bauer said.

'We need you if we can trust you,' Rich said.

Again Bauer grinned fiercely. 'And there's only one way of settling that.'

He spun his horse, and rode hard onto the Logan Cut.

An hour after leaving the ox-bow, with the trail and Flats Creek still as close as two rattlers in a courting dance, they got further confirmation that they were heading in the right direction. Unfortunately, bad news came with the good.

The sound of a shot came to them, muffled, but not too far away.

Matt Danver's sharp young eyes were the first to spot pin-points of yellow light across the flat land a little way off the trail to their left. As they drew closer, they were revealed as lanterns bobbing a couple of feet above the ground some way in front of a low house the windows of which were in darkness. Closer still and raised voices reached them through the warm night air, and it became clear that the lights were lanterns held by two men.

'A man and a boy,' Danver said, again picking out details before any of the others.

'Could be nothing,' Brown said, 'but why would a man take his son outside in the dead of night.'

'A mare foaling?' Danver offered. Then he frowned. 'If so, they've got troubles. Those two have walked away from the corral, and if there is a mare there she's on her own and lying awful still.'

Then, as they rode up, the light from one of the lanterns glinted on metal as a bearded man turned to face them. He called out loudly, in harsh tones that yet held a hint of tremor.

'Hold it there, whoever you are. Put your hands in the air, hold tight to the stars.'

'There ain't no moon, there ain't no stars,' Danver muttered, and he began to shake in his effort to hold back laughter.

'We're a posse out hunting two men,' Brown called. 'I'm Deputy Vern brown, of Mesquite Flats.'

He swiftly unpinned his badge and held it high to reflect the light of the lanterns as the man approached, covering them with what looked like the biggest rifle in Arizona. The boy, about fifteen years old, hovered in the background. He, too, was carrying a rifle, what looked like a skinny .22.

The man held the lantern above his head, but the rifle's muzzle was perceptibly lower.

128

'I know you,' he said, and now the rifle was lowered all the way as he stepped close to Brown's horse. 'Know you, and that feller.' He nodded at Bauer. 'And I reckon I know all I need to know about the fellers you must be chasin'. Damn pair, they wrecked a couple of poles opening up the corral, took a couple of horses and let the rest run free. Left one of theirs behind, real lame. If you heard a shot, that was me putting him out of his misery.'

'Kris Bauer and Al Ferris are the two we're after,' Brown said. 'If you know me, you should know Ferris.'

'Know the kid, know his pa too, more's the pity.' The man shook his head, at the same time managing another baleful glare in Dieter Bauer's direction. 'That who it was? Don't know what you're after 'em for, but add horse thief to the list and when you catch 'em, hang 'em high.'

'I'll remember that, Caxton,' Bauer said, and Brown flashed him a look.

'They carry on up the Cut?' he said, turning again to the man called Caxton.

'You betcha. Here and gone before I was out of the house.'

'How long ago?'

'An hour, maybe. But I keep good stock. On fresh horses now, and with a change of mount there for them when the first's wrung out, you'll have your work cut out catchin' up.'

'Doesn't follow,' Danver said. 'With a horse each on a trail rope, they'll be slowed down some. Pullin' those horses after them's taken away the advantage they gained from stealing your prime horse flesh.'

'In that case,' Vern Brown said, 'we'd best ride like hell, make the most of what could be their first and only mistake.'

SIXTEEN

It was a long, hot and tiring night. The stubborn moon lurked behind thin high clouds. The Logan Cut and Flats Creek kept parting company, then cosying up again like fickle lovers. The one faint sign that told hard-riding Bodene Rich and his companions that they were not the only men alive in the whole of western Arizona territory was the occasional whiff of hanging dust. As they passed through yet one more in a succession of twisting arroyos, that dust would be there in their nostrils, acrid, faint, but enough to convince them that they could hear the iron hoofs of ghostly riders echoing from the rocky walls.

The first suggestion that they were gaining on their quarry came when the sun was no more than a line of glittering gold along the eastern rim of the Gila Desert. Suddenly, out of thin mist that was unrolling like a moth-eaten grey sheet from the creek's flat waters, two unsaddled horses came cantering. They ran straight on by, ears flat, eyes knowing but untroubled as they stared ahead to where an unseen man with a rifle waited with his hand on a boy's shoulder.

'Heading for home, and a heap of fresh oats,' Danver said with a grin as all four men drew rein. 'Been set free, recently, I'd say. Now what does that tell us?'

'Ferris and Bauer switched horses, let two of 'em loose. They're panicking, they can feel our hot breath on their necks,' Brown said.

'How so?' Rich was frowning in thought. 'If that's true, they must've been using glasses to watch us from a distance – which is just not possible during the hours of darkness. The other answer is we're close enough to be seen with the naked eye, and they're now running for their lives.'

'At this point I'll come in with a word of warning,' Dieter Bauer said. 'If we're getting close enough to threaten 'em, those boys are not going to run; not Ferris, and not Kris. If I were you, I'd be waiting with a lot of trepidation for that fatal shot to come winging out of nowhere.'

'What about you?'

Bauer grinned at Brown. 'I'm here to stop you shootin' at them. If they're going to be doing any shooting, it won't be me lined up in their sights.'

The first shot came when the dazzling morning light was causing their vision to dance and Bodene Rich was fourth man in the string as they rode the Logan Cut between a steep bank on one side and a broad, shallow stretch of Flats Creek.

Rich's mount reared and spun away from the over-grown bank as a brittle rustling announced the presence of an angry rattlesnake. The horse's reaction saved Rich's life. The bullet clipped his mount's flying mane, hissed on through and kicked up a glistening plume of water. It was followed by the vicious crack of the hidden rifle. Then, as horses and riders milled in confused disarray, a shot from a second rifle on the other side of Flats Creek punched a hole in the crown of Rich's Stetson.

'On, push on,' Rich yelled and, controlling his horse with the strength of arms and thighs, he spurred forwards.

Danver and Brown caught on fast. Bent low in the saddle they kicked their mounts into a gallop, pulled clear and were away along the narrow strip of trail that was turning them into trapped and exposed sitting ducks. Deliberately or through confusion, Dieter Bauer hesitated. Roaring his anger, Rich drove his horse through the narrow gap between Bauer and the steep bank, almost dumping the rancher in the creek.

Looking ahead, Rich saw Brown streak past Danver and swing his horse towards the water. He had seen a section where flat gravel lay just below the surface, and he tore across the creek leaving in his wake a fine spray of droplets glittering like jewels in the sunlight. The far rifle cracked again. Brown flattened himself along his horse's neck. Then he was all the way across and urging the roan up the short steep bank and on towards the trees where the rifleman lay hidden.

The first gunman had chosen his spot with the intention of making his first shot count. Ahead of Rich and Danver as they pounded down the trail the creek turned lazily to the right. Set a couple of hundred yards back from that bend a low rock shelf lay in front of a stand of cottonwoods from which the sun had not yet lifted the mist. The gunman was tucked in between rocks and trees. He had a clear view straight down the narrow section of the Logan Cut, but fate had decreed that his first shot would miss. Now he was hidden, but had given away his position and was trapped.

'Split up,' Rich yelled.

The space between the high bank and the creek began swiftly to widen. As it did so the bank swooped down until there was nothing but an expanse of flat, hard earth stretching into the distance. Taking advantage of the space, Danver swung left. Rich followed the creek to the right, and suddenly the gunman had two targets, both of them pushing hard out to his flanks. Seeing the danger he snapped a wild shot at Danver, a second at Rich. Both missed by a mile.

Has to be young Kris Bauer, Rich thought. *Ferris would be unfazed. He'd take his time, make every shot count, make sure he drew blood.*

He was thinking those thoughts and planning his own approach when gunfire rattled on the far side of the creek. Rich thought he heard a faint cry, of agony or despair. Deputy – or gunman? If he was right, and Ferris was over there, then Brown could be in trouble.

Then, as another shot from the gunman holed up behind the rocks whined perilously close, he dismissed all thought of the deputy from his mind. Hanging low, Indian fashion, on the right side of his horse, he raced on, reached the end of the stand of cottonwoods and dropped to the ground.

In front of his face, a bullet kicked up dirt. Spitting, rubbing his eyes, Rich rolled towards the misty trees and into cover. His horse had continued for a further twenty yards, then halted, quivering. Rich's rifle was still in its boot. To go for it now would be too risky. But. . . .

He removed his holed hat, risked poking his head out from cover, narrowing his eyes in the ever-brightening light. From his new position he could see along the gap between rocks and trees. On the edge of the mist the gunman was exposed, and no more than thirty yards away – within six-gun range. Unable to look in two directions at the same time, he'd been forced to turn away. His back was towards Rich as he watched Matt Danver. Danver was still in the saddle. He'd swung wide around the gunman's right flank, then turned towards him. Now he was coming in hard and fast. His six-gun was spitting flame.

The recklessness of youth, Rich thought – but, by God, it was working. The gunman was on his knees. He seemed paralysed, frozen to the spot. Bullets were chipping sharp splinters from the rocks. Rich heard

him cry out, clutch his face. Then, hastily, as if real-
izing he had to act as Danver thundered down on
him, he lifted his rifle.

Coolly, calmly, Bodene Rich stood up, drew his
Colt and fired a single shot. The pistol kicked in his
hand. There was the solid, meaty thud of lead hitting
living flesh. The gunman stiffened. His back arched.
Then he twisted awkwardly, fell face down and lay
still.

There was a hot, heavy stillness. It was mostly in
Rich's mind, and was broken like a bad dream by the
sudden splash of cool water and crunch of wet
shingle as a horse was ridden into the creek, the hard
drum of hoofs as Danver rode in.

'Was that you or me got him?' the wrangler called,
drawing rein and tumbling from the saddle.

'The crazy way you were shooting, a barn door
would've been safe,' Rich said.

Danver flapped a hand in disgust. He ran to the
fallen man, dropped to his knees and flipped him
over – then looked up at Rich as he walked over.
There was something in his face: surprise, and
expectancy Rich couldn't understand.

'Looks like my shooting really was wild,' Danver
said, still watching Rich. 'I sprayed him with bullets,
missed with every damn one. That's bad news. If I'd
plugged him, nobody could've accused you of shooting this man in the back.'

'Why would anyone bother?' Rich said – then
stopped abruptly as he caught sight of the dead
man's face. 'Jesus Christ,' he said softly. 'That's

Erskine Thackray.'

'Don't tell me how those two got ahead of us, but we got ourselves bushwhacked by a couple of raw Easterners. They were hunting down the man they believe killed this feller's brother. That's you. And the way it's worked out could make you look real bad.'

'A back shot, with only you and me here to explain.' Rich nodded. 'A lot's going to depend on what's happened with Ed Thackray – it had to be him across the creek. That's Vern riding in now. He's alone, which tells it's own story. And if Ed Thackray's dead. . . .'

Brown was riding up from the creek. He was looking away up the trail to his left, then frowning and shaking his head.

'Where the hell is Dieter Bauer?' he called.

'You know, that man went clear out of my head,' Rich said to Danver. Then, as Brown rode in, he said, 'I thought he was following us, but keeping well back from the action.'

'Me, I thought the only reason he rode along was to stand between us and his boy.'

'Yeah, but his boy's not here.'

'Did he know that?'

Brown had pulled up and was sitting slack in the saddle. There was the blank, withdrawn look in his eyes a man gets in bad situations, and Rich knew from the deputy's demeanour that the older Thackray was dead. He flapped a hand vaguely.

'I guess Dieter was quicker on the uptake than any

of us – and quicker still to move when he saw us all tied up and the way through wide open.'

'Well, we know where he's gone,' Vern Brown said, 'and we know why. Now, 'stead of three of us chasing Kris and Ferris with Dieter along as some kind of holy goddamn mediator, the odds are down from three on two to evens.'

'But one of those three's a brutal killer, twice over,' Matt Danver said. 'I guess there's no argument Bradley Shaw's killer also killed Pete McReady's pa?'

'None at all,' Vern Brown said. 'And that's why, for Dan's sake – or maybe this should be for Pete, now – we do this right. Dieter Bauer will be a tough nut to crack, but whatever happens we're taking Kris Bauer back to Mesquite Flats to face a judge. A formality. He'll hang for his crimes, and I for one will be there to watch him kick.'

SEVENTEEN

Knowing they were using up valuable time, Rich and Vern Brown brought together the dead Thackrays, father and son, on the Logan Cut side of Flats Creek, and scouted around for enough small rocks to cover the two bodies. They laid a scattering of dry brush-wood over the burial site, then stepped back to view their handiwork.

'Needed doing,' Brown said, 'case we ever have to come back and recover the bodies – God forbid.'

While they were working, Matt Danver had gone after the Thackrays' mounts. He located them easily enough, and when he rode back in he explained what he had done.

'Unsaddled 'em, and took 'em to a patch of grass by the creek. Some shelter there, too. They're unlikely to move far, and if we come back this way we can pick them up. . . .'

With nothing to tell them otherwise they were forced to assume that Kris Bauer and Ferris would stay with

the reasonably easy terrain afforded by the Logan
Cut, with Dieter in hot pursuit. Rich, Brown and
Danver thus had no option but to go with that conclusion and push blindly along the trail in a
north-westerly direction, nursing their horses while
coaxing from them all possible speed.

In that manner the morning sped away, lazily
crossed the blistering heat of midday and became
sultry afternoon, and in all those monotonous hours
of dusty pursuit they caught not one glimpse of their
quarry. Though little was said, glances were
exchanged many times, and to Rich it became clear
that all three men were seriously considering the possibility that they had been outsmarted. If that was
true, then Ferris and the Bauers were running free; if
they had left the Logan Cut and forded Flats Creek,
they would now be nothing more than faint specks
lost anywhere in a thousand square miles of feature-
less desert.

It was in Rich's mind to call a halt and rest while
they considered their options, when they heard the
flat crack of a pistol shot. It was followed by a second,
and almost immediately after that there came the
deeper boom that they knew had to be Dieter
Bauer's shotgun.

'There,' Danver said, the young kid with sharp
ears and eyes who had instantly located the gunfire's
origin. He was pointing to his left, away from Flats
Creek. The land rose steeply, but not too high. As
Vern Brown swore softly, spurred his horse off the
trail and sent it crashing through the short dry scrub,

140

the unseen six-gun cracked twice more, the flat echoes fading away into an aching silence that was like the haunting memories of a dying man's last breath.

The three men reached the uneven crest of the rise strung out in a line, and took their horses over the top with Bodene Rich at the rear eating dust. They found themselves descending into a shallow basin where the sun was trapped and the heat rose in waves to take away a man's breath. Rich tightened the reins, holding his mount back a little so that he could survey the scene, judge what they were likely to be up against if once again violence flared.

And why the hell wouldn't it, for God's sake?

At the basin's centre a coyote's yellowing skeleton lay in the hollow atop an immense slab of flat rock. Alongside the rock, Al Ferris lay flat on his back with his arms flung wide. His chest was a mess of torn, bloody flesh. His white eyes staring sightlessly at the sun. Kris Bauer was a short distance away. He was slumped against a boulder. His eyes were closed, his face as grey as a rooming-house sheet, his shirt front glistening with bright red blood.

Close to where he had fallen, the low rock ledges forming the rear of the basin fell away to a narrow gap through which could be seen a view down a long, grassy slope. The three horses that had carried Ferris and the Bauers to the basin were resting in the scant shade afforded by the slight overhang in a looming rock face away to Kris Bauer's right.

Roughly midway between the two downed men,

Dieter Bauer stood watching Brown, Danver and Rich as they rode down from the rim. One foot was raised, planted on the slab of rock. His shotgun was held, butt on thigh, muzzle pointing at the dazzling skies. Two six-guns jutted from the waistband of his pants.

Dust billowed as Danver and the deputy thundered to a halt. As Rich rode to join them, Brown tumbled from the saddle, whipped around to face Bauer. Danver took one look at the bloody mess that was Ferris, then rode over to dismount by Kris Bauer.

Bodene Rich sat still in the saddle. He was still studying the scene, but now recalling what they had heard, what had drawn them there; the sequence of shots; putting a story together in his mind, piece by piece. But it was guesswork, he knew that. So he watched, and waited.

'What the hell happened here?'

Dieter Bauer scowled at Brown.

'What I expected, what made me ride on ahead, what I was hoping to stop. Al knew you were after 'em, knew that for Kris the game was up. He tried to get my boy to go back and face the music.'

'You admitting he's guilty?'

'There's no use denyin' it. He's my son, but if he's gone bad—'

'So the two of them fought it out? Ferris doing the persuading, Kris having none of it and reacting with violence?'

'See for yourself. Ferris was too good. I got to 'em when he'd gunned down my boy. I'd say Kris got one shot off, but it went wide and that was the end of it. Ferris's shot hit him square, knocked him off his feet.'

'Then you used your shotgun to down Ferris, took his pistols,' Rich said.

'Damn right. I did what any father would have done.'

'When we got here,' Rich said, 'you were standing as you are now, out in the open like some goddamn Mex bandit. Shouldn't you have been over there seeing to your boy? Shouldn't you be there now, 'stead of jawing while he bleeds to death?'

'I told you. My boy died when Al Ferris's slug pierced his heart,' Bauer said.

'No,' Matt Danver said. 'He wasn't then, and he isn't now. Someone bring a water bottle. He's got a throat as dry as an old Mex serape, but he's struggling to say something – and from what I can make out, the bullet that downed him didn't come from Ferris.'

It seemed, to Bodene Rich, that Danver's shocking words raced like flame along a short fuse to ignite the explosive mixture of intense emotion that was bottled up in Dieter Bauer's bulky frame. There was an instant's pause. Then Bauer jerked as if hit by a punch, and with a terrible throaty roar he leaped away from the slab of rock and charged across the basin's dusty floor.

Danver's eyes widened. Like a cat, he sprang to the side and rolled out of the rancher's path, instinctively lifting his arms to protect his head. But the heavy weapon Bauer was now holding by its twin barrels was not intended for the wrangler. Bauer slammed to a halt. The scattergun whirled, came across in a vicious, horizontal blow carrying the weight of the rancher's shoulders. The heavy wooden stock crashed against the side of his son's head. Kris Bauer's head snapped back. There was a terrible splintering sound as his skull cracked sickeningly against the boulder. His mouth fell open, his eyes rolled, and he slid down the rough stone face to lie in a crumpled, inert heap.

Time seemed to stand still. Seconds hung motionless. The hot air became an intolerable weight, adding lead to a man's limbs. The only person in the basin who was unaffected was Dieter Bauer. As a stone dislodged from the boulder by his son's dead weight clinked onto the gravel, he flung the scattergun with its shattered stock at Vern Brown then made a run for the horses.

The spell was broken. Bodene Rich whipped out his six-gun and snapped a shot at the running man. But Bauer was not to be stopped. His run became a crouching scuttle, as fast as the fastest of land crabs. Rich's shot screamed over his head and smacked into rock. Bent over, Bauer snatched a six-gun from his waist-band. His first shot took Vern Brown in the right arm. The deputy spun, then dropped in agony. Bauer's second missed Rich but clipped his horse's ear. The animal reared, squealing in pain. Rich hung on to the horn with one hand, but his pistol flew into the air as he grabbed for the reins with the other. As he fought his mount, struggling to stay in the saddle, Dieter Bauer reached the standing horses and leaped onto one that had a Winchester rifle jutting from the saddle boot. Using the strength of his arms he lifted and turned the animal's head and spurred straight towards the opening in the rocks.

Matt Danver was climbing to his feet, fumbling for his six-gun. This time he was Bauer's target, and he was too slow and unbalanced to leap out of the way. The racing horse bowled him over, and stamped on him with a pounding rear hoof. An instant later Bauer was through the basin's walls and racing down the long, raking slope.

Dust settled as Bodene Rich's horse calmed. Danver climbed to his feet clutching his ribs, then limped to the opening, squinting in the bright sunlight as he watched the fleeing Dieter Bauer. Vern Brown was standing unsteadily. His hand was clamped to his right arm. Blood dripped from his fingers. His face was white, his teeth clenched and jaw muscles hard knots. As he glared across at Rich, his eyes burned with rage.

'So now we know,' he said tightly.

'Like father, like son,' Rich said. 'You see the way he swung that shotgun? Damn it, they're both left handed, him and his boy – but what he did there proves beyond any doubt it was Dieter who knocked down the Booths, Dieter who killed Bradley Shaw and Dan McReady.'

Suddenly, unexpectedly, a shot cracked. Rich half

turned, frowning. Matt Danver was still staring away into the distance. And Vern Brown was still talking, furious with himself as he realized how they'd been fooled.

'He came with us, not to protect his son from what he described as a ruthless posse,' the deputy said, 'but to make sure he kept his mouth shut.'

'Caught up with them, Ferris and Kris, and Ferris must have taken one look at him and known at once what would happen. Hell, of course he did, that's the reason he helped the kid get away.' Rich's face was grim. 'So Ferris stood tall and tried to take Bauer, and it didn't work out. He missed with both his shots, and Bauer used the shotgun to rip him apart; both barrels, so there could be no possibility of a mistake.' He nodded across at the dead youngster. 'It's hard to believe, but the two shots we heard after the shotgun blast must have been Dieter shooting down his own son.'

'And this time he did slip up, because he didn't finish him off.' Brown looked across at Danver. 'You said Kris was trying to talk,' he called. 'Did he manage to say anything to you?'

Danver was on his way back across the hollow. There was a look on his face Rich couldn't fathom.

'Not that I could hear with any clarity, but in the end he didn't need to, did he?' the wrangler said. 'Dieter Bauer's guilty of assault, and murder, and he'll pay the price.'

'When we catch the bastard,' Brown said, 'and if we don't move mighty fast—'

146

'Oh, we'll catch him all right,' Danver cut in, 'because I can tell you now he didn't make it all the way down the slope. His horse stepped in a hole, snapped its leg. That was the shot you heard – seems Bauer had more compassion for an injured horse than he did for his own son. Put it out of its misery, and right now he's holed up in a stand of trees that wouldn't give cover to a frightened jack-rabbit. He's there for the taking.'

EIGHTEEN

There had been undisguised excitement in Matt Danver's voice when he said, 'Oh, we'll catch him all right', so it was hardly surprising that when Bodene Rich insisted he stay in the basin and well clear of any action, his face fell.

'You're badly shook up,' Rich explained. 'Bowled over by a running horse, then stamped on. Hell, I'd be out of it myself, that happened to me.'

'Yeah, but you and Vern, you're—'

'Old?' Rich grinned. 'Don't say it, kid, or your condition will suddenly become much worse. Besides, Vern's staying right here with you.'

Brown was in no shape to argue, Rich judged, but well capable of pulling his weight from a distance. He had a rifle and, once it was up against his shoulder, his wounded right arm didn't have to do much more than lift his hand to the trigger. He could post himself against the basin's edge, lean up against the rimrock, look down the slope to watch the fun and rip off a couple of well-aimed shots if Rich got into difficulties.

Danver, still grumbling, moved alongside the deputy.

Although he'd been fighting to stay in the saddle when Bauer made his getaway, Rich had seen the rancher fling himself onto the horse carrying the Winchester. He guessed horse and rifle had belonged to Ferris. And Ferris would have made damn sure the rifle's magazine was fully loaded. So, despite Danver's assertion that Bauer was there for the taking, Rich knew that wasn't the case. Bauer was in the trees, and a man armed with a rifle doesn't need that much cover when he's facing an opponent forced to shoot from a distance with a hand gun.

Which was where the wounded deputy started to earn his money, Rich figured. To make the six-gun work for him, he had to get in close. To do that, Bauer's advantage had to be nullified.

'Vern,' he said, 'when I get 'bout halfway between here and where Bauer's holed up, I want you to start laying shots into those trees. Spaced out. Accurate. Don't waste shells. Put every shot close enough to part Bauer's hair, make damn sure he keeps his head down.'

Brown nodded slowly, but his eyes were thought-ful, and it was clear that he wasn't happy.

'And I've changed my mind,' Rich said, sensing possible dissent. 'Matt, I want you out there on your horse. I want you to ride a wide loop that takes you out towards the Cut and Flats Creek, then back in on a tight curve, real fast. To Bauer, it'll look as if you're aiming to come up behind him, take him from the rear.'

Danver grinned. 'But what will I really be doing?'

'Just that,' Rich said, 'if I don't make it. Ride in, shoot the sonofabitch, if necessary in the back. But my guess is it'll be all over before you get there. Vern will be pumping bullets into those trees, and Bauer will be going cross-eyed as he tries to keep his head down and watch both you and me at the same time.'

Vern Brown looked at Rich, smiled apologetically and shook his head. 'I see very little wrong with any of that,' he said carefully, 'but as the only man in the posse carrying a badge I've got the authority to make a change if there's room for improvement. And there is. It's a good plan. It stays unchanged. But I swap places with young Danver.'

'Why?'

'You're asking for accuracy with the rifle. With this right arm, that's something I can't guarantee.'

'Riding down there favouring that arm, you could fall off your horse.'

'And your horse could break a leg. Bauer's did.' There was a stubborn set to Brown's jaw. 'Both men who ride out there are going to face danger. The danger comes from Dieter Bauer, who's got a rifle and Ferris's six-guns and will be fighting for his life. There's no guarantee the two riding out are going to come out of this alive – but with Danver here working that rifle, we know there's a guarantee of good covering fire from a young man with first-class vision and a steady hand.'

'Yes, but—'

'Also,' Brown said, 'why risk a young life when there's a couple of old fogies who won't be missed? Secure behind these rocks, with a rifle—'

'OK.' Rich nodded, grinning. 'I get your point – though I'm not saying I appreciate the description – but if we don't make a move soon, Bauer'll die of boredom or old age.'

'Feel in danger of that myself,' Matt Danver said, 'so how about this from the youngest member of the posse: why the hell don't we all mount up, ride down there and storm the bastard?'

'Because,' Bodene Rich said, 'I think Bauer's got something nasty up his sleeve.'

He had no idea where the thought came from; it leaped unbidden into his mind, and hung there like unknown menace hidden in a dark shadow. And as he and Brown rode out through the gap in the rocks leaving Danver on watch, he was gripped by a fore-boding so strong it felt as if he had eaten a pound of rotten meat and was paying the inevitable price.

NINETEEN

Once clear of the basin and out in open country, Rich and Brown split up. Brown veered to the right and commenced riding the wide loop suggested by Rich, while Rich himself sent his mount galloping arrow-straight down the slope towards the distant trees.

He was well aware that Bauer was a dangerous opponent. The loss of his horse might have left the rancher on foot, and vulnerable, but attackers bearing down on opposition firing from cover were nearly always at a disadvantage. The only exception was if they had vastly superior forces and could overwhelm the defenders – and here that wasn't the case.

Rich had ridden scarcely twenty yards when it was made clear to him that he'd at made at least two mistakes. The first was in telling Brown – and by default, Danver, who'd taken his place – to start firing at Bauer's position only when Rich was closing in on the trees. That turned out to be too late. The second was in underestimating Bauer; in believing that the

152

man would lie low until he could see the whites of his attackers' eyes.

Rich had gone no more than thirty yards when he saw a bright wink of a muzzle flash in the trees; and when, head down into the wind, he glanced to his right, it was to see Vern Brown knocked clean out of the saddle. The deputy hit the ground so hard he bounced. Then he lay bunched and still and, with pricked ears, his mount trotted away, reins trailing, stirrups flapping.

Rich's first thought: Matt, use your common sense. His second, as Danver did just that and opened up with the rifle, was to wonder if the cause of his terrible foreboding had come and gone – or if the worst was yet to come?

He had no time to worry, or start counting his grey hairs. The big horse was eating up the ground, the stand of trees was looming ever larger, and Matt Danver was doing a grand job of keeping Dieter Bauer pinned to the ground.

Hope flared within Rich. He swerved around Bauer's dead mount, pointed his horse a little to the right. The slope eased. Suddenly he was on flatter ground. Holding the horse at breakneck speed, he dropped a hand to his holster and loosened his six-gun.

No sign of Bauer. Close up, the stand of trees was revealed as sparse. So . . . what should he do? Crash into the trees? Risk getting tangled up, with no way through and Bauer grinning at him along the barrel of Ferris's Winchester? Or drop out of the saddle and roll in the open, hope the horse would draw Bauer's fire.

He was out of time. Without conscious thought he hauled back on the reins and slid from the saddle. As he fell, he slapped the horse hard. It veered away, head high. Rich rolled, rolled again, all the time keeping his eyes on the trees for any sign of Bauer.

He was up and running at a crouch when he heard a hoarse yell of triumph and an object flew through the air. It was spinning, trailing sparks. And it was flying high towards Rich's horse, which had slowed as the reins began to drag in the coarse grass.

Then there was a bright flash, a tremendous explosion. Bodene Rich was knocked off his feet. There was an eerie sensation of flying through the air. Then he hit the ground hard, and all around him the world turned black.

'He stood up, showed himself for about the first time,' Matt Danver said. 'He was leaping like a crazy man. Forgot all about me. I thought he was going to do a war dance through the trees, finish you off with one of those left-handed swings he's got so good at. Maybe that's what he had in mind. But we'll never know. I put a bullet through his brain – like hitting a pea, I'd say – and it was *adios amigo*.'

Rich took another drink from Danver's water bottle. He was sitting up against a tree, fingering his torn shirt and absently listening to the fading ringing in his ears. The stick of dynamite with its sputtering fuse would have killed him if it had been thrown in his direction. But Bauer was in too much haste – and too aware of Danver's steady fire – to realize that Rich had dropped from the saddle and was coming at him from another direction. The horse died. Rich went to sleep and awoke with a headache and bloody nostrils. A small price.

'There's bodies stretching all the way along the Logan Cut from here to Mesquite Flats.' He thought of something, and looked questioningly at Danver. 'What about Vern.'

The wrangler shook his head. 'Killed instantly.'

'Damn. So if Pete McReady hadn't stayed in town, there'd be nobody left to explain what this was all about. And when the dead are counted, I reckon there'll be a heap of explaining to do.'

'So we take the bodies back with us,' Danver said, 'give us something to add weight to our story.' He grinned at the macabre image.

'Three bodies, two horses,' Rich said. 'What do we do, walk?'

'Ride double. Three dead men strapped on the other horse. Be uncomfortable for 'em, but, hell, they won't complain.' He caught the water bottle as Rich tossed it to him and climbed stiffly to his feet. 'And when we get back to where you planted the Thackrays, there'll be two fresh horses waiting and we'll be out of the woods.'

TWENTY

It was another hot, dry day. The wind was moaning faintly across the flat, fenced slope on the outskirts of Mesquite Flats that was the town's cemetery: Boot Hill. It was picking up dust and driving the gritty particles against the worn stones and warped wooden crosses, and causing the flowers Ellie Bauer had placed on her son's grave to dance and toss their heads. Despite the solemnity of the occasion, the sight brought a smile to Ellie's face.

Bodene Rich touched her shoulder, smoothed her jacket gently with the palm of his hand.

'You always knew it was Dieter who had almost killed Red Booth, didn't you?'

'Of course. I overheard him one night. I think he must have been talking to Al Ferris, because of course Al was in it, too. And then I told that fine man, Bradley Shaw, and I suppose that was the start of the trouble.'

'The start of the end.' Rich nodded. 'Dieter ambushed Shaw, the prison warden, but by then it

156

was pointless locking the stable door because the horse had bolted.'

'You.'

'I was out, yes, and Dieter's days were numbered – though at that time most people thought your boy was guilty of . . . well, assault, then Shaw's murder.' He lifted an eyebrow. 'How did Dieter know you'd betrayed him?'

Ellie smiled. 'Betrayed? What a strange word, considering the state of my marriage.' She lifted a hand, let it fall. 'He knew I was seeing Brad; had always believed, wrongly, that we were more than friends. Anyway, perhaps he overheard me, in turn; put two and two together; or simply assumed that's what I had done, and knew he had to strike first or he'd take your place in Yuma.'

'And what people were seeing – what you were seeing in Kris was not guilt, but nervousness that was rapidly turning to fear. He knew his pa was vicious, ruthless, devious, knew he'd do everything he could to shift the blame—'

'And I'd lost Brad and could see the writing on the wall, and so I got out.'

'But now you're back,' Bodene Rich said softly.

'I came back to bury my son.' She shook her head, was silent for a moment. Then she said, 'And with Dieter gone the Booths are back at their place on the creek, of course – but you are still homeless.'

He shrugged. 'Not for long. Rebuilding's not hard, and I've got Matt Danver to help me.'

'Just about everything's wrapped up now, but I've

been wondering about the Thackrays. I was the first to bring you news of their arrival on the scene, wasn't I? But were they justified in pursuing you? Did you kill your partner, Ed Thackray, and walk away with a fortune?'

'I've no idea who murdered Ed. I did walk away with a lot of money, because we were covered by partnership insurance and I sold a profitable going concern.'

'And your name?'

'I was Dean Rickard. Now I'm Bodene Rich.'

She smiled. 'I like it. It has a much nicer ring.'

They turned away from the fresh grave and walked towards the gate, Ellie a little ahead.

'You said rebuilding's not hard, but it does take time. Where will you live in the meantime? You and Matt?'

'As far as I can recall, the fire didn't reach the bunkhouse, and there's plenty of room there.' He caught up, looked down at her and asked the question he knew she was expecting. 'Why do you ask?'

'You know why. I've got a house with more than one empty room. It's just across the creek from BS Connected. If you thought perhaps that Matt would be uncomfortable sharing rooms with the boss. . . .'

'I tell you what,' Bodene Rich said, again touching her shoulder but this time leaving his hand there. 'Why don't we talk about that as yet unspoken invitation over coffee in Millie's café? The arrangement would be perfectly proper, you'd see to that, but you need to know if you can stand to look at my ugly face

158

each morning across the breakfast table.'

'And you?'

'Well, if you're referring to your face,' he said, 'I've known for some time.'

And with hands that were perhaps a mite familiar, he helped her onto her horse and together they rode the short distance into Mesquite Flats.

Library Link Issues (For Staff Use Only)

1	2	3	4	5	6	7	8	9
		336A	488A					